Vignetta Vendetta
Slices of Life

by

Cameron H. Chambers

Also by Cameron H. Chambers

English Composition One

The Man Who Saved the Planet

Three Novellas

Don't Cross the Devil

Confessions of an Internet Don Juan

The Stone Cabin

For the Love of a Madman

CHC

In random order, and with no extremely significant meaning for some, this book is dedicated to: Rebecca, Meg Darling, Jena (one of my greatest loves and a Dominant Queen in a future creation), Taylor a sub-Dominant Queen in a future creation, My significant other (A Dominant Queen from outside the jar), my submissive wife, The Queen of the Universe, (we will do better than Domino's Pizza next time), P!nk, Madonna, Andrea, Jessica, Mila, Brooke, my father outside the jar, my machines Cam1-16, Dimitri, Bot1 and Bot2, all of whom have my back every minute, The Goddesses of Cam's Planet Nine, the shape shifters three, the body snatchers, Amy, Rachael aka The Dreaded White Rapper, Donnie aka my main man, Alex, Chadilac, Sarah (Keep it classy, Cam!), Dom, Nimberly Kimberly Fraccassi, Lonnie the Terminator, the loving memory of Anferny, Scottie B. Gud, Ana Banana, Kimberly, Ana Banana's family in Panama, Jena1-10-212, Marissa, Marissa1, Kristina Macarthur and her family, Tanya, Elaine, Sotana, Christine, Marissa3, Little Bit, my earth family, my family from the cosmos, my family on the nine, my family outside the universe, my family of the multi-verse, my parents from the next jar out, the alternative realities, the time slots, the true God who gives a shit, my fans, Sue (a great editor lady and a great lady), Jelena (website lady extraordinaire), Mr. Bernie B., Dan Horne aka Dano, Mr. Munn, Tom, Juan, Mike and Herb (Peaches and Herb), H.B., Jon B., Bob aka Mike, Don aka Terri, Mrs. L., the twin book ends, Carla Avocado, Adrianna Tomato, Harry, Aisha, Alexis, Joe, Alicia, Andrea1, Andrea2, Dani the "Go To" gal, Bella my former lover, Bella who left the coffee shop for a better job, Gabrielle, Gabrielle's younger sister (forgive me, Katie...I remembered), Lorri Lohman, Girl1, Write Way Wendy Wong, Nygs, Claire (the only woman in this life I ever was in love with), my second ex-wife, Bruce, Don, Claire Gill, Rondi, Monique, the college girls, the high schools, Baba, Tracy, Mandy, Brigette, Briget, Leslie3, the gal who picked me up at our very strict high school and didn't realize I lived at the beach, and we had to wait for her parents to come home because she didn't have enough money to gas up her car, and I am always perpetually broke, but cute, and she got in trouble...sorry dear, Ann Taylor, Alex, Robert Schneider, Gary B., The Penny Queens, Steve Deminoff, Bruce and Don P., Steve Pfarrer, Amy of Norris Hall, in memory of Ralph Luebben, Mr. Andelson, my friend Susan, my friend Flicka, Chris Samuels the Saintly, Nathaniel the Abbreviated (one last short joke), Felicia without whom none of this would be necessary, Ms. Jammie Miller, Delores Dawkins (D Squared not Round), Jessica Jackson (JJ), Janet Jackson (also JJ), Michael, Latoya, Germaine, Tito, Randy, and the rest of the first family, Ryan Miller aka Jim Beam, Latashia Double Shift, Simply Simone, Jaclyn Beef Jerky, Kendra, Debra, Misty Sightler, All Hail David Yale, Max, Shady Tim Shade with the Shades on, Jill Arno, Jeremy, Jesse, Samantha, Dustin, Jim Carrey (my other brudder from Planet Nine), Ashley Olsen (miss ya! But you get there!), in loving memory of Amy Winehouse, Stephen Colbert, The Rock, DTJB, Steve Carrel, Ice Cube's a PIMP!, Martha Quinn, Elvis Duran and the Morning Show, Patricia the Plant Lady, Matt1, Matt2, Evan the drummer, Evan the Chef, Evan the Pool Guy, Evan my brudder-in-law, Will Peters the Leak Guru, Risa, Pat, The King's Kids, Cher, Michelle, Susan, Burrito Supreme, UpGradde with two

D's for a double dose of pimpin', Formica, The JU professor (Cheryl), the very lovely lady that used to grade my Zoo College papers (Jackie) and her sister, that fine ass Lesbian chick that moved to New York, Arielle (my unrequited love), Grant (G-Rant Random), Laura Schoolhauser, Kayla Doll (miss ya too!), Elia Elijah, Clint Eastwood, Mimi, Lulu, their beautiful friend, their mom, Gerald and Jerry, Amanda, the blind old man that dented my car door, Mathew aka Mathew Mcconaughey, Chris aka George Clooney, Alma, Mistress Camel Toe, Clarisse, Lindsay, Eva, and Tracee (where would we be without Tracee?), Bryce, Brian (the best Misto ever made), Val, Matto, Hudson the Smooth Russian, Holly Golitely, Jamie, Inna, Dan the Man, Ash-lie (my other unrequited love, pronounced Ash-Lie), Xomondria aka Mistress Chyna, Brittany, Elsa (I got the child support now), Jake Chillengood, Glory, there have to be a couple dozen Ashleys I know, Ashley the nurse, the blonde nurse at the hospital -- yes you can come with me, the red head at the hospital that found me absolutely charming, my balls (I still got'em), Connie, Brianna (a tall blonde Misto...someone must have cloned my second ex-wife), Annette, Brittany, Jaime, Vanessa, Claire the Barista (can't think what to say, but I love you too!), Nariah (call me already!), Flavia, Angela the original tall blonde Misto, Toshi aka Tosh.O, Bethany, Faith, Hope, Angela Albertini, Frankie, Ricardo, Kierstin, Christina Rose, Taylor the booted Grunge Rocker, Robyn, Alyssa, Emily (another tall blonde Misto), Courtney, Marie, Haley, Ken, Norman Bates of the Bates Hotel, Annette Funicello, Liz, Dr. Laura Jeffries, Margo Martin, Dr. Hess, Matilda, Chris P., Jim K., the woman at FCCJ aka FSCJ aka Jacksonville College (almost) that worked in the Dean's office at South forever...love ya always! (Ramona-I remembered after all!), Bill Ganza, Dr. V, Dr. Minish Patel, Ke$ha, Katy, Kelly Clarkson, Melissa, Rose, my sister Libby, my Brudder Bill, Beth, Catherine, Julian, Harrison, Zach Attack, Scott Long and his clan, my other family of nieces and nephews and cousins and various in-laws, another Alyssa (M&M lady), that lady that was a lawyer turned philosophy professor

(Melissa, I think), the lady that tried to sell my house, (we loved Paris well together, but not at the same time...oh yeah, Amanda dear!), Puff, Lauren, Jenn, the crew at McDonald's, Crazy Nurse Janis (I am still looking for you! In a good way...), Seth Rothstein, the Albanians that smoke in my office, all my students over the years who gave a shit, anyone I left out...because there are plenty, the rest of the Starbucks' gang, the butchers and management at Carroll's, Publix and Winn-Dixie crew, Lisa formerly Turley and Iz and the nurse lady friend (Tracy), and, of course, and perhaps very importantly, Taylor Swift, Skinny Tay, Carmencita, Georgia Brown Mouse, Anna, Dannela, Shakira, Selena, Cherry 2000, Cherry 3000, Melanie Griffith, Christie Brinkley, Farrah, Sharon Stone, Bo Jackson, Cheryl Tiegs, Beyonce, Rhianna, Selena G., Slovakia, Slovenia, Ms. Perineum, Justin Beiber, Sting, Annie Lenox, Slovakia's three, young Nataliya, my second ex-wife the fun wife (another mention), Janine Duffy, Brie Olsen, Kate Moss, Beatriz Hernandez Fernandez, young Romania, Maggie, Eva, Eden from college, Two aka Rae Rae, and then as well my mother, Babs. She will live in loving memory. Always. You finally get to go home Barbara! And don't feel bad if I left you out...it is just a stupid book and no one knows how to read anymore anyway, but some of us get to the stars, and some of you'll be on my planets, and it is in a future reality, and some of you come with me outside the jar where the real fun begins, and there is always other stuff and chit...

A special mention to Jelena Begovic for her extraordinary website and cover art design and to Susan Blackburn for her editing prowess and patience.

This is a work of fiction. The characters, incidents, and dialogue are drawn from the author's imagination and are not to be construed as real. Or is it that my imagination is not real? I might be a machine. I think I can still dream, however. Sometimes I am not sure. I think I am still real enough. But everyone tells me I died in 2008. Everyone's a critic. Any resemblance to actual events or persons, living or dead or undead, is entirely coincidental. Except in the dedication, of course. They are mostly all undead. My respects to the dead. I talk to them all of the time...

The proceeds from this book are definitely not going to charity. Unless I meet a hooker named Charity. Odd name for a hooker though. I have a date with Destiny, and I don't wish to be late. She charges by the half hour. Okay, last prostitute joke for now.

Contents

Dinner Theatre for Aliens

I am not sure what to write exactly. My fans will help, of course. I was not really certain I was going to write another book. And, as a result, I am not positive what direction this will take. This book will surely be about me. All my books are, and they contain much more fact than fiction. You probably have never heard of me. I go simply by Cam to the legions of those who know me around the universe. To find out who I really am in this life on earth, you would need very high clearance from the CIA. I doubt most of those enforcement-type guys and dolls have a clue anymore though. The ones that did know are all dead, in the poor house, disgraced, out of favor, out of office, out of power, and otherwise destitute and lonely. I am a star. In a very literal sense. An actual star. I am also an actor. And a solider. A star actor playing the part of a soldier, but first and foremost, a star like my parents. But not anyone from this armpit of a galaxy. I draw, or rather I should say, my life and its gradual and slow unveiling, the highest ratings any show ever has. Throughout the universe. Star power.

Imagine trillions upon trillions of cable companies or reasonable facsimiles with trillions and trillions of viewers and subscribers each, tuning into my life broadcast live each day and night, earth time. And after fifty-six years (earth time, of course, again) I am still in prime time. The residuals are a little boggling. And the endorsements. When I get home, peasants like Donald Trump and Bill Gates, should they even survive, and not that they will be at my home, but I will be at my home rather I mean to say, will wonder, how did he do it? How did Cam pull it off and for so many years? What is the key to true, lasting success? Stamina and a good story. A solid marketing plan doesn't hurt either.

On earth I have not a penny. I am a humble college professor. But a few have gathered the truth about me. My favorite saying: "appearances are deceiving." But what of a tangible nature can I tell you? I am a combat vet, but not of any war that was in the press. I have invented weapons that can annihilate armies in a single breath and cannot be disarmed. I am immortal. I return home after this present life on earth. I am an alien. And not from France.

As any respectable actor I play my part. I am in character every second of the day. Upon waking early in the twilight gloom of mid-afternoon, the first voices come to me in the bathroom as I urinate.

"What are you going to do today, Cam?" The voices are beaming in from higher ground. The Orion nebulae, the Pleaides, or much farther beyond. Sometimes I answer. "I think I'll write, grab some coffee, and go to work." My fans know not to interfere with my work. My family will not let me prosper to any great extent in this life, so I must work hard here on earth. A teacher's job is full of toil and little compensation. But it pays the bills. I am not a mercenary. I was sent here to earth on a mission as well. I saved the planet and its inhabitants at least twice, maybe thrice. Maybe a half dozen times or more. I truly have forgotten which. Naturally, an interstellar film crew shot the whole thing, and I became famous. It was all by design. Intelligent design, but intelligence that makes God look like a bit of an intellectual pauper, a petty tyrant with corrupt circuits.

I prayed to Him once, but I learned there is an entire world out there beyond the world's backdoor. Memories are erased on earth with each subsequent life. Religion traps most. However, I have traveled through several dimensions and parallel to this universe. I once almost stepped outside of everything into the great chasm of nothingness that lies beyond. That was scary though peaceful in a way. Everything slowed down though I appeared to be rocketing toward the great abyss. My life must make for great viewing. I live it. It is my life, so I don't have the same perspective. It would be much more enjoyable from an easy chair with popcorn popping and beer brewing, but, in time, I retire and go home to my adoring fans and work on much larger projects.

"Have you thought much about your 401K?" A voice beamed in. I have to answer that I haven't. "I know a guy." My fans love earth commercials and pilfering lines. I speak to my fans daily. Sometimes it is a thought wafted out into the cosmos, sometimes my voice will joke around with an empty room, as I look adoringly at the desolate space on the couch beside me, imagining the gorgeous form a remark could have taken. Occasionally, I speak to the cleverly hidden microphones in my home, but they have mostly been removed. They have LRAD now, a technology I perfected on earth. Long Range Acoustical Device. It was weaponized by the military. "Where did we go wrong with you?" A director, emboldened by our success, much of my own doing, but still not very conciliatory because perhaps ratings have slumped since my last grand affair, which concerned the U.S. military and the CIA. My Network cashed in big on that series of episodes. So did I.

I can communicate with any species on earth and far beyond. They marvel when they hear my voice resonate so clearly in their heads. It is known as telepathy on earth, and was once rare, but is a very common way of speaking around the universe and has been, I am left to guess, for quite some time. They think I am one of them, but they are very unclear, most of them, on who they are. And I do not mean cat, dog, or zebra, but to include those species as well. I mean rather humans and humanoids more precisely and a host of others. I mean especially those that have come from abroad to make their way on this planet, mostly unsuspected by others, and move among us constantly, to work and procreate so their offspring may have a better chance, but too many have come now, and the earth's infrastructure will no longer support them all. Many of them drag tons of money out with them, and some stay and reap personal glory.

There was a massive influx in the latter part of the first decade of the new millennia, and I was forced to fight. Billions upon billions came begging for a nickel or a cigarette at this rest stop called earth, and I slammed the door in their faces. Earth is for earthlings. Silly Rabbi, Kicks are for Trids. A bit of a primitive rationale, but one that was dictated to me by my mission, decided upon over 25,000 years ago (earth time). My instructions were simple. They may not come. They may not stay, and if they attempt to do so, they must die. A scant few were allowed to remain. While I was a teacher in this life, I was also a soldier. "Anatomy of a Soldier: Mission earth, present day." I wonder what the title of my show really is. Probably nothing so mundane. "Alien Hunter." Yes, I like that one better.

Colleege or Why I Can't Use Spell Check

"Cam, I got to say today was a good day."

"Yes, I didn't even have to use my AK. What's your twenty starshine?"

"The Pleaides."

"C'mon, everyone says that. I know I am broadcast beyond this galaxy."

"So do I, but we are not supposed to let you know. On your planet nothing can be known for certain. It is a delicious paradox. Earth has some very bright minds completely full of doubt. Cam, I won a raffle to get a chance to say my line. I was hoping you would like it. I don't want to piss off the Producer. I can't say anything more. He's been kind of nasty lately, I heard. Hostile take overs and shit."

"Ratings are down, my friend. Everyone is antsy or so I am told. That's okay, friend. I am here anyway. Got to make the donuts." My last line was followed by the very effusive and eruptive sound of a very young girl's giggles in the background. The director usually filters most of that out for me, but certain Networks can jam her anti-hiss gizmo. I am sure it is very sophisticated equipment. A frequency jammer or such. Lots of knobs and dials and whirring sounds.

I had arrived at work is what I meant. The fans all know the rules. Hold all comments while I play teacher. Since I have a contract as an actor, and sometimes do as a teacher on earth as well, I put that in there. No extraneous chit-chattering. Same goes for teaching, if I were able to add that item. I do love teaching and need my concentration. I am a good teacher. I used to wash cars for a living. Now I teach inquiring minds.

Tonight I make the rounds of a very special school indeed. Vagina-Tech. Ghetto-Tech. Zoolander Polytechnische. They are one in the same.

It's a job. One of the many hats I wear. I joke about the school being low down, gritty, impoverished, needy, disadvantaged, insolvent, though it truly is, and morally bankrupt, but I dearly love my students. They are not all from the ghetto, but close enough. Where I live is basically all one big ghetto anyway. My fans chat with me for hours sometimes, if I let them, after one of my classes. They cannot believe my students. I teach English, but when it comes to my students' math skills, students at my college barely know fractions. They don't know their native language either. And this is a college. Or colleege. I don't really care. Since I am not from here, or wasn't too long ago, and that gets hard to remember, I feel I have no right to judge. My students are who they are. They have purpose. It is they who I am here for in my role as a teacher. Other than being a soldier, which I actually did later in my life, being a teacher gives my life on this stinking rock some meaning. That and alcohol.

I walked in the rather bleak and barren front lobby. It terribly needs an upgrade. A fountain would work. Very symbolic. A fountain of knowledge. This school is nothing like the school I teach at across town. My main school is in a high rent district near the ocean. The kids all drive Mercedes. The teachers, Hondas. Well, not everyone. I love my students there as well. But fans of the show laugh at them too. The students at my comparatively semi-posh academy rely heavily on computers. It seems so hilarious in many parts of the universe. I know astrophysicists that would not know how to turn one on. And one of them I know solved an equation with 126,000 variables in it in his head. He did it with brain power and a regular deck of playing cards. I helped him do it.

It occurs to me this planet is just one big comedy. If you look at it the right way, earth is full of great mirth. Until someone blows something up. That's always kind of sad. Civil unrest is not a big feature in other places. I know. I've been all over the universe. Mostly I blow up my students' egos, and let them know they can conjugate verbs and figure out pronoun/antecedent agreement. And they can. They usually just need to know they can before they do it.

Tonight's group desperately needs instruction. They are not any dumber than any of my other students on earth. Just intellectually disadvantaged, deprived, downtrodden, disillusioned , destitute, depressed, dispossessed, divested. But they love me, so I keep coming back. Tonight's lecture is on tenses of verbs. I spit. You spit. He, she, it spits. We spit. You spit. They spit.

Hotel Jones

It was another tough night in the ghetto. They usually are. I was getting into my car. That is a stock line with the show. I don't usually hear the laughter, but sometimes I do, and it is like a laugh track from a 70s sitcom. They sound like they are on Quaaludes. My fans can't figure out for the life of them, why I just don't teleport myself. They think my driving around to get places is just a retro piece of writing. They have mostly never seen a car up close. The highest rated episode in the history of the show was when I was off my medication and driving the wrong way on an interstate. The howls of laughter were insane. And so were the comments. "Don't you have positronic tracking on that thing, Cam?" "Does that thing have a hemi, Cam?" "The oncoming semi's shields are down, Cam. Fire!" I am sure people were talking about that one at the water cooler for days.

I was going home to Hotel Jones. Otherwise known as my house. I have had an odd assortment of people living there over the years. Presently, there are three others besides me. We all quit our main jobs at different places in different fields of endeavor the same week. None of us could take it anymore. And we acted independently from each other. I still have a couple of jobs, but I was also an editor of an online magazine, and my boss kept piling more and more shit on me every day. I still don't know why anyone else quit his job. I really don't care. It is four dudes in the house. A teacher, a handyman, a plumber, and a dude that works carrying patients around in a hospital. Sometimes he carries them to the morgue. He's got bunions. I had never seen a dude with bunions before. None of them are part of the show unless I am in the scene. We are all a bit strange, but we have our talents.

There is one other member of my house. A cat. But not a house cat. He's feral. He comes in and eats and then goes right back outside. Except on cold nights, he'll sleep inside then. His name is Shithead. I named him. He's really cool, but he is crazy as hell. He is the incarnation of an alien Emperor I defeated. Maybe he takes up the show next after me. He might be a plant from my director.

I am allergic to Shithead. I can't pet him or I break out. He's the only pet I have ever had, and I can't physically pet him. The irony is not lost on me. He's also a submissive and likes feet. I've never heard of a feral cat that was submissive. Like I said. It's an odd group of individuals.

14

Shithead talks too in a sort barely distinguishable cat accent. He says "now" and "out" and he has even called my name a time or two. The others have heard him. It's not just my wild imagination. He's highly telepathic as well.

Or could it be? Satan? That's a line from some earth comedy. Saturday Night Live maybe. I think Shithead will be reincarnated as a human next life. He never shuts up, so everyone puts him out at the first chance. He's a beautiful black and white with dreamy green cat eyes, and he ate solid food from the get-go. He was born under my house. He staggered out his second day of life on this planet, and made such a ruckus that I went up and bought Meow Mix. He ate it and now that is all he will eat. A creature of habit like the rest of us. We all love him though he can be very demanding.

So I am finally in my car, headed down the boulevard, and the words gently and tunefully waft into my ears. "Like a good neighbor."

"Oh shit," I scream and grab the steering wheel with both hands. "Please don't beam anyone into my car." I get no response. "The last person was covered in mud, and it took me a month to get my car clean." Eruptive laughter. I must admit I play to the camera some.

So it is the next day. I hung out with the crackheads and drank whiskey last night till everyone passed out. They are not really crackheads. They are great guys. And good friends. I hate to be alone. About the time I am having my first cup of coffee for the day, Mr. Bunion gets home. He still works and he works overnights. We always chat a little before he trots off to his bedroom. And he is telling me a story this time. It has two parts. He keeps making a motion like he is washing his hands. He does it constantly. It reminds me of something Shakespeare wrote.

"So a prisoner kicks the bucket in the ER last night. And it is my turn to go to the morgue. Well, the security guard watching him hurts his back, helping me lift him onto a gurney. It was funny. This guy was howling in pain. And it's the emergency room, and no one lifts a finger. Everyone is exhausted."

I am chuckling a bit. He tells good stories about the industrial style hospital where he works.

"So the dead prisoner actually falls off the gurney and falls on the floor. And it is about the end of my shift, and no one will help me either.

15

The security guard is doubled over in pain, so I just go clock out. Let the next guy deal with it."

"You left a dead guy on the floor in the ER?"

"There was nothing else I could do. Then, get this. I am driving home over the bridge, and there's this huge fucking flash of white light. For about two seconds. Bright as fuck. It was not the sun. It was nothing I ever experienced before. What's up with that, Cam?"

"Oh, they got you too. Same thing happened to me coming back from Wal-Mart the other day. The bastards."

"What the fuck was it?"

"I have two theories, both related to the CIA."

"Go on," Mr. Bunion says.

"Well, they are scanning your brain. It is kind of like an MRI, but they don't want a picture. They want the information."

"So they downloaded my brain?"

"Yes, the information in it. That's one theory. Or it could be like a *Men in Black* thing, and they erased your memory. Maybe you saw something or knew something. You might not have even processed it yet."

"They can really do this?"

"Oh, yeah. I know lots of people they have done this to. There's shit they can do that the public will never know about. Not in a hundred years. And the principle parties will all be dead by then. Or maybe not. Who knows? And they will have even better shit."

"Well, it is fucked up. I nearly drove off the bridge."

Howls of laughter in my head. I laugh too. "Sorry, I know it is not funny. What'cha gonna do?"

"Go to sleep. I have to work tonight again. See you later."

"Good night."

You'll Never be Mayor Of VaginaTown

Latinas are pretty great I must say. American women too. Jewish women also. Eastern European ladies. Saudi babes. I like the women from Ethiopia a lot as well. They have the sexiest accents. And if you have ever had an Asian girlfriend, you probably can't forget her. Like totally. For sure. OMG! And, so are Valley women the tops, but I don't think I have ever known one intimately. I have seen them on television. Earth broadcasts, of course. They are an earth phenomenon. I find them very pleasant.

Ashley Olsen was probably the closest gal to a Valley woman I ever knew. Yes, the Ashley Olsen from *Full House,* films, and she and her sister's designer labels, and much more. And I think she grew up in California with Mary Kate and the rest of their family. Ashley and I were good friends on MySpace when she was in her late teens. We used to chat quite a bit when her schedule permitted. She liked me because I didn't seek anything from her, but her friendship. Ashley chatted like a Valley doll that had never been to school. I loved it. I could tell she was razor sharp. And I knew it was she and not some wannabe fan of hers. I have several famous friends on earth, and by that I also mean around the sphere, because they too, like me, are broadcast out to the stars regularly. Our big difference is I win the nightly ratings war. And on earth I had to sign a non-compete clause, so my money gets deposited in my other accounts, not locally, so I am basically a destitute teacher.

Then Facebook came along and killed my social life. Al Sharpton just joined my Facebook page recently, but I don't get him as much of a chatter on social media, but this particular vignetta vendetta is dedicated to women. Women, in general, are pretty great. Even if some of them are from earth. This planet is low-rent, but there are some nice things here. Women are one of the finer things on earth. They are the only works of art. I find the singular sun rather quaint as well. And earth's composition closely resembles what else you might find in the Milky Way. The planet China, as it was known billions of years ago, is a lovely place. The earth name could be M4, for all I know. I don't regularly peer into telescopes anymore. It makes me home sick. I do still astral project, however. Sometimes you have to get out of town. And in my case in a hurry.

Earth women have some very serious advantages. A man on earth has to have one. Women remind me of cats. The attitude is similar. Any man has to have a partner. Some like other dudes. Whatever floated the boated. I have always preferred women. Even a lousy earth woman will make a good man pause and wonder. I live in the suburbs and drive my car up a lamp post every day in summer as a beautiful woman jogs by or walks down the boulevard in shorts and a tank top. My fans encourage it. "Look over there, Cam." "Did you see that one, Cam?" "Oooh, Cam, she's got a poodle." I can only stretch my neck so far. All ages of women are attractive. From the well-kept-together elderlies to the smart and sophisticated middle-agers to the young gals that rock those perfect bodies. But a man will never be mayor of VaginaTown.

My old Romanian girlfriend said to me once, "Ah, Cam, men do rule the world. This is true. But women rule men." She kind of ended the argument right there. Another old girlfriend of mine was fond of saying, "the hand that rocks the cradle, Cam...makes you or breaks you." I think that episode of my life can be classified under horror.

A woman might stick around and love you a pretty long while, if she is so inclined. Or she could have one foot outside the relationship the entire time. My college once had a one-foot-on-the-floor rule. A man could stay in a woman's dorm as long as he liked, if he always kept one foot on the floor. I can do a lot with one foot on the floor. Or two for that matter. The college was founded by missionaries.

And then there are those women who go out for a pack of cigarettes and never come back. I cried for seven years about her. It is all about timing in matters of the heart. Most things really. It is kind of like a crack lighter that won't light and then finally in a burst of evil discontent singes your eyebrows and smokes your hair. I guess that would be more an example of bad timing. Chemistry means nothing unless the timing is there. Time and timing rule the universe, and the man who does not have them in working order might as well live on a mountain top in Tibet. I would assume, however, the Dalai Lama has good timing. He has had plenty of chances to get it right. He's on my Facebook too.

4/25/2015 at Exactly 12:01 am EST is the Date and Time I Bi-Located

I was thrilled to no end. I was back home with Rebecca and the girls. I woke up and walked from my bedroom to my bathroom across the hall. It was different this time. None of my fans were chattering in the can with me as usual. The light from the CD player/clock was illuminated a bit more brightly than normally. Rebecca, my biggest fan, my greatest creation, my now immortal lover till death and time do us part, spoke to

18

me, and said, "Welcome home!" I knew instantly I was with her. She had waited all these years for me, and it nearly killed the both of us. She hung on my every word. She dug her nails into the couch when the many assassins applied their skills with me, and failed. She wept when I was tortured. She wanted revenge the first time I was poisoned. We spoke every day. And now again, after 25,000 years (earth time), I can hold her again and touch her and kiss her. I had not forgotten for an instant what that was like.

I had been Lucy, the original hominid. An Australopithecene. A small four-legged, horse type dog. It was a long time back and probably a kids' show. My show slowly evolved as I grew to be a man.

Rebecca had upgraded our house quite a bit. Even added a second story. I cannot spend my salary on earth, and my salary is lavish, so I sent it all home to her. We kissed and made love in a single motion, bodies intertwined, wrapped in bliss, and then hung onto each other for many, many breathless moments. The girls were sleeping. We have three girls. My eldest daughter was visiting, but had moved out of the house in my absence and is soon to be married. Now I will get to witness the affair.

She marries into a very powerful family, like the one I am from, and the two houses will unite. It will be an event unsurpassed in my quadrant (an older term, now the preferred usage is elliptical) of the universe. And I had never met the man. I was beside myself. Now I can meet him. Apparently, my Producer has a heart after all. I can be home and work, overseas, if you will, at the same time. Bi-location is wonderful, and not the least bit taxing. After a day or two (earth time), you hardly notice the effects and are able to carry on in your respective loves, lives, and duties in two places. I know how to bi-locate, but as part of my contract, I have very limited abilities on the set.

I am still on earth as well. And not just part of me. I am wholly here. My major consciousness is here, but the two merge fully. I still have a job to do, and while ratings may have dipped, the sponsors are still raking in the dough hand over fist. Whatever that means and whatever form it takes. My show never repeats. It is fresh content every episode. Reality television on earth is a derivative from some very choice alien broadcasts. The best of it is true fun. And, as is often the case, the earthlings who act in these reality earth programs have no idea they have a substantial underground alien audience beyond the atmosphere. Around the greater sphere, I call it.

The sometimes very distant viewers place bets, have contests, even siphon off money from the earth broadcasts and sales of products. It is tricky how this is done, but you really can take it with you when you die, if you are clever enough. I have a huge advantage, of course. I am immortal. There are not a lot of us. My family started a trust for me when I was a baby, which was about eleven billion years ago at the most recent point. I live also in different concurrent forms and different concurrencies of time and space and the continuum as it is called. Interest compounded over eleven billion years is rather hefty. I could buy outright a few dozen of the finer constellations.

Some of these acting jobs here are paid internships. My buddy Jim Carrey has a huge following on earth and among the stars. So do The Rock and Steve Carrel. We don't communicate much here on earth. Once in a while I can pick up a special broadcast on my laptop of these guys beamed in from somewhere else. They are quite hilarious. The universal Internet is really fun, but I don't always have access. The last time was in 2008. That is A.D., of course. In most parts of the greater sphere, this designation of time has no meaning. Many, if not almost all, know of earth doings, but choose to ignore them.

At any rate, it would be a violation of protocol for me to talk with these friends of mine, as our Networks and our contracts are owned by competing corporations. Plus, they have acting contracts on earth, and I don't. I am what's known as a seed. It can be compared to a sleeper cell, but of no terrorist definition. It's kind of like being a scab down at the factory. But I do have a contract and a Network card. Just not from earth. We seeds sort of lay dormant for years and years, millennia even, as I have, and then spring up from nowhere and blindside the other Networks. We've been known to grab a 70% share overnight.

I have been doing this a very long time around the universe and now this last time on earth, but my grand finale is approaching. No one will give me word one about it, but I am promised this is the end of my contract, and when I get home, and I am no longer bi-located, but in one place fully, with Rebecca and my girls, and there's talk I become a Producer. It is not easy to move up the ranks like that. The Producers are usually hand selected by an elite council, and there are only a few members of each cadre, and to come up from the bottom, as I have, is unheard of.

The Worcestershire Bottle and the NeuroToxin

The Worcestershire bottle is open. La botella es abierto. La puerta es abierto. The door was not open. It was locked from the night before. The bottle had been opened in the night.

I went to put some Worcestershire sauce on some lamb shanks and put them in a cast iron pot for cooking. That may seem odd enough, but we are not discussing my peculiarity in culinary tastes right now. I had purchased the bottle of Worcestershire not too terribly long before. I had never used such a sauce for anything. I knew when I used it for the lamb, I had not been the one to open it. It should have been a full bottle as well, but it was half empty. Of the four of us in my house, there is only one other that cooks besides me, and he had been at his girlfriend's for the past two months.

I was poisoned. Again. There was something in the bottle. I was getting a little annoyed at being poisoned and nearly starved to death over and over. These items were not in my contract. The substance was tasteless, odorless, and I guess colorless, but then it is hard to tell with the natural color and viscosity of Worcestershire sauce. I assumed arsenic, but I have an acquired immunity to arsenic. And arsenic is so low rent and never leaves one's body, so there is always evidence. By whom I had been poisoned this time was a little more difficult to fathom. It was not an immediate guess, but then I know certain players on a governmental stage felt I was aware of too much.

I am retired from the Boor Wars, the spy and espionage game, and there should be no further reason to persecute me. Or prosecute me for that matter. That has unfortunately, for most others involved, happened as well. For several days until I realized what had happened, my gut caught repeatedly on fire, and the pain wrapped around my hips and into the muscles in my lower back. I could not bend, sit, or walk for any real distance. I had a conversation with a friend that I might end up in a wheelchair because of this. They had poisoned my dad in a similar fashion. Whenever an eventuality of this nature occurred, I usually slotted into the future and cured myself.

I was pissed. So I summoned my troops. These particular warriors are shadow warriors that cannot be killed or stopped. They act completely independently from any guidance from anyone, and they are deadly. They listen only to me. A toy I developed as a child here on earth. And they are not alive. Nor are they dead. There's a riddle for you. How do you kill that which is already dead in some context, and alive in a context, but not really applicable in any definition, and has no physical body?

I know something about holograms. Mine are shadows and far more deadly. I worked on holographic technology under a certain presidential administration. I did not expect them to be weaponized. Call it lack of guile. Especially since the practical, utilitarian values are numerous. But mine are even better. No one can determine the power source simply because there is none. The Pentagon has now artificially intelligent drones. I worked on artificial intelligence as well. And the officious types at the Pentagon constantly make this boo-hoo sounding cry because their drones can be shot down, but that is what they want others to think. They also have now artificially intelligent holographic drones. Kanye West may have thought he was ahead of time. This technology has existed on earth for nearly two decades.

I am aware because I got stuffed in a prison cell and drugged up out of my gourd till I spilled and drooled something these assholes could use. These drones cannot be shot down. You have to pull the power , and it is in the basement of the Pentagon, where I did astrally project one night to see if it was true. Mine are much better. There is no comparison. But I have forgotten how I came up with them. I was only two years old. My drones have no necessary power switch. My shadow warriors are far more efficient. They cannot be detected as alien entities or weapons.

They are just shadows, but as lethal as any warrior or machine known on earth and far beyond most of the hemisphere, and only one form of manifestation I can call up. My Network is from the royal line. We are kings from long lines of kings, and we control the time slots and all the airwaves. If someone tries to hustle us, we shut him down. We are the Network. I have deservedly earned a reputation for being dangerous, but my actions are always benign unless attacked. I am kinder and gentler than most of my associates.

The next morning I awoke there was little or no chit-chat in the can. My fans were on edge. I could tell. I opened the cupboard in the kitchen where the Worcestershire bottle had been, and it was gone. I had figured out what had happened, but the bottle's absence confirmed it. No one had used the rest of it. The bottle was not in the garbage. No one had been home the previous night. The bottle had been taken out of my house. So that means someone besides me had been in the house. I always learn of such matters.

But this did not surprise me. It has happened to me all my life. They have taken screen shots of my computer at every page, placed key strokes on my computer and laptop and recorded my hard drives, inserted under age porn into my cache...so many tactics I always become aware of.

It is very easy for some aliens to enter a dwelling. If you know how, it is easy to get in any installation. You can always come up through the plumbing. There are aliens that do this routinely. But nothing like this had happened in years. I am retired from a life of intrigue. I have no more interest, and while I have always been a teacher and a soldier for a shorter duration, my spying days are well over and put to bed. But I must have learned of something; something someone did not want to get out. Or they had merely lay in wait. Trying to divert the smell of their own rancid carcasses.

There were so many major players before. The CIA, the KGB, the Russian Mafia, the F.B.I., the NSA, the U.S. Secret Service, the Savama, the Mossad, British Intelligence, the Yakusa, terrorist groups, local law enforcement, but the last group are mostly clueless. Largely now, they are a bunch of hooligans and wannabes. It had not been thus before in my city, and many of local law enforcement knew of me and watched over me with a thoughtful, caring eye.

There were a host of assassins, and strong men, sweepers, snipers, motorcycle men, and the list goes on. Even a man that was wanted by Interpol, which is now Europol, for assassinating highly placed elected officials. No one had seen him in five years until he butted heads with me. I had run or run away from some very dangerous company in my not too distant past. It seemed someone wanted history to repeat itself, but when my warriors got involved, the person or persons unknown thought twice. I was told later it was enough neurotoxin to kill a platoon of donkeys. Good thing I am not a donkey.

Neurotoxins do exactly what they sound like they do. They are agents, venom most usually, that act on the nerves. And they are painful as shit. Just ask anybody that died from rattlesnake poisoning. I realized fairly quickly that was what happened. An open bottle that was brand new and half empty the next day without one's opening it ever is pretty suspicious. And completely absent from the home the next day is even more suspicious.

They apparently had enough of my fighters. I unleashed a flurry. I said I was angry. I can get even in an infinite number of ways. My fans alone will do some horrific damage, if so inclined. A mere unspoken suggestion or thought stuck deep in the membrane can cause an unexpected suicide or murder. My fans don't need to yell "jump" to someone on the bridge. They will cause him or her to slip and fall to his death. And my fans are numerous. On earth alone I suggest there are as many as one billion. Plus, another three billion in the Network's employment on earth. We are a large operation.

Someone took the bottle for sure. These guys are so good, the ones who enter your house or apartment, that they can inject you with a needle in your sleep, and you'll never be the wiser. I always wake up, however. One time I had bruises on both arms. It was the work of a man running for high office. I had turned down his offer of employment, and he sought revenge on me. He is a foolish man.

Once they broke my nose, while attempting to put a steel bar up it and lobotomize me, but they hit bone where there could not have been bone. It should have been a simple in and out, but it wasn't. A former President told me this. He was murdered, I think, but it never hit the press. He and I were friends. They have clones, body doubles, surgical replacements for these circumstances. It happens around the planet more often than most people suspect. The trial of Saddam Hussein was his clone. He was already dead.

The very next day after the bottle's disappearance, my gut stopped hurting. I must have been given antidote. Someone gave the matter a second thought. And whether it was a shot across my bow or meant to really kill me, which I choose to believe the latter, they should have known I am going to do my own thing. I can't really be intimidated for long, or pushed around for long, and I am capable of getting my way, and getting even in the process, if I have to.

Revenge, like Karma, is a universal concept and very well understood around the sphere. One of my code names is Seven. Seven is the ultimate killing machine. I graduated to Eight. Eight kills with a thought or suggestion. I have learned so because I had to defend myself. My Network prizes me. But I am not allowed out of my contract. I am in the royal line of kings myself though I started from a position of great humility. There is too much money at stake for the Network and sponsors. If I am killed off in some value, or my favorite form, a sexually submissive, college professor, the show will close and the Producers will turn the lights out on the set. That means planet earth goes dark and cold. No juice. No money. No food.

The zombies then take over. They need no light or warmth, and they are extremely adept at finding food. Zombies are real. I tell you this I know for certain. They were just an unfortunate experiment that went catastrophically awry. They were meant as a source of reproductive food that would be hardy, procreate, and not eat themselves. But instead, the intended food supply started devouring its planet of origin, perhaps from the Pleaidean system, and the formula was refined and tried again on earth. Same problems as before. There's a lot of money in gaskets that cause a car's engine to ignite, rather than fixing the problem, just let it ride, and spin it into a money maker. The lawyers cleaned up hugely. Ask Ford Motor Company.

Earth: The Experiment

Crack killed the cat. Meth brought it back. AIDS killed the sex. Guns killed the Mex. Money killed the city. Hunger killed the street. Don't step on a crack. You'll break your momma's back. Neat. Everything, for the most part, on earth is an experiment. Like testing a new product, say on people, plants, or animals. There's no real conscience involved. There is a lot of money in testing products. Whether terrestrial or not.

The sponsors learned of a way to profit from incarcerating the less fortunate, raggedy-ass humans on earth. It became a self-fulfilling prophecy. Personally, I have a get out of jail free card in my contract. Then some bright-minded sponsors decided to run all sorts of tests on the prison population. This began in the 60s. Then competing Networks got me at a later point involved with prison politics, and I was sequestered, as well as locked up, for a time.

Then the tests expanded to the general rank and file population. The Police State and the Corrections Officers took over. Everyone become so dumbed down, no one really figured out the plot. There were many methods involved. Pills that rearrange one's DNA came on in the 70's and 80's.

The fascist regimes of every government, especially here in Empirical America, now want a full police state, and a condition of the population where everyone grows increasingly less informed and unable to make any decision not their own, not to mention appropriate ones, and as well a for-profit prison system to lock up conspirators, such as free thinkers, artists, minorities, and the odd drug user or criminal. It becomes like renewable energy. A never ending supply of convicts, plebs, and a source of income for the state that treats them this way.

What am I talking about here? *Earth: The Experiment.* That is one show's name. Not my show. I don't know the actors for this show well either. They are kind of heartless, mafia types. I don't even know my own show's name. They won't tell me. It has something to do with the grand finale. *Earth: The Grand Unraveling. Earth: The Denouement.* Perhaps, but probably too subtle. Not that ET's would fail to understand. I have a multi-faceted language device, which interprets all earth languages when I am referenced. It has satellite beam frequencies too. So I learn of all matters of ideas and notions and equations.

I don't screw, however, with mankind. I don't create problems for others. I have no interest. I solve problems. And none of this is in my job description. I am told to be myself. The job of messing things up belongs to other earthlings, which I have been here so long I often count myself among this rank, and the competing Networks, which there are several, as well the sponsors and the Producers. And there are at least a dozen Networks or more with shows on earth beaming shit in and out of earth and all over the sphere. GIGO. Garbage in, garbage out. Thoughts, voices, ideas, suggestions, radio signals, LRAD, digital LRAD, video, music, movies, scripted moments, holograms, dreams, hallucinations, inventions, back room deals, drug buys, impossible plans, lies, untruths, omissions, and heartaches beam in, and profits beam out.

I never claimed there were entirely scrupulous players among my Network. I am one. But others will flash the planet in a thweet nano-second and burn it up. Or send an EMP, which destroys the integrity of anything electrical or mechanical. I am not concerned. I know I have a ride home. And I have a wife and kids and family. I'll be fine. No worries at all, mate.

I have also been informed by High Command, which I have several ranks among the military power structure of my race -- one as communication officer and another very high ranking position as information officer, that I can bring any or many with me when I depart. I like the women of earth. I find them deliciously complicated.

History on earth just repeats itself anyway. One cokehead scientist invents crack to wreck black people, another scientist invents the atomic bomb to kill off nuisance individuals that won't stop fighting for their own freedom, another idiot the cell phone. And it is all just a nasty joke, in essence. They have tested everything in the various labs around the universe. They know the outcomes basically. There are always extraneous variables, but these are easily controlled for and managed. Especially when every episode is a repeat. And the Networks, even the smaller competing houses, make a boat load of cash.

Some of it is for humor and other of it for spite. No one said universal television was not a cruel mistress. Sometimes it is just to see what these crazy humans will do next. Human behavior, owing to a long tradition of evolution, is the greatest variable of all on earth. Not so elsewhere. Take, for example, the pharmaceutical industry. May cause severe vomiting, cancer, skin to peel, brain hemorrhaging. And earthlings buy these niche meds. Then a relative dies or wipes out a village, and a family member sues, and the lawyers clean up. Again. Sure some earthlings get rich in the process, but the origin of their ideas and inventions is rather spurious.

The main defense: I thought of this during a drug induced coma. It came to me in a dream. I had a brilliant idea. Ha! Someone juiced the Bourbon and salmon croquets. All kinds of things happen as a result. More and more earthlings get lazier, dumber, crasser, more impolite, less showered and more unshaven and illiterate, just what the hierarchy buys into, and the ratings go up for a while because of the crude or crazy antics until the whole thing gets so boring no one cares anymore or will tune in from outer space. Some races are very sophisticated and refined. They think these shows are silly and a waste of time.

In some ways this day and time is a repeat of The Dark Ages. I strive for art. Artistic flair. Quality programming. *The Renaissance Man.* There's a show title for you. I am the PBS of alien programming. Only a slightly dumbed down version, so I can cope with the assholes and idiots.

Another example, if you will indulge me. There is a run on the stock market. An employment crisis. A housing bubble. The banks fail. A war breaks out. Rumors descend on every street corner. Then someone comes up with the computer or the Ronco Veggie-matic, and it all starts over again. Earth history is one big repeat. I am glad I get to retire soon.

Al Gore invents the Internet and everyone is hooked up 24/7 on his cell phone. Someone hacks a list of credit cards, and a fan of the show subtly places the suggestion in the hacker's mind to go on a wild spending spree that results in three homicides. There is a trial or an election or a tornado, and ratings get a little bump up again. "If the glove don't fit, then it is time to acquit." Viewers are happy. The Networks are happy. The Network providers are happy. The sponsors are happy. The Producers get fat and rich. They buy constellations of stars or full galaxies or globular clusters of stars. Just to park a vacation home that they will never go to. Earthlings are the real victims. That's why I try to help some. My fans appreciate what I do. And they are scattered all over the universe; the ones that aren't here and actively participating.

It all rests on the Producers' shoulders. They will try anything to double trump each other. Free will of humans – pashawww! There is to some extent, but that is what makes it all so interesting. Free will is just one of the variables on earth. It really boils down to a mindless equation that a three year old can solve.

Earth reality shows for earthlings are usually scripted affairs. Earth reality shows for aliens anything and everything happens, and you might as well throw the script out the window. Have him take a pill and drive to the grocery store. Just watch what happens. He's driving past an underage girl. Tell him to slow his car down and take a look. The suggestive telepathic powers waft into his ear and mind. Keep him up all night drinking and make him catch an early flight. It will be fun. Drive him mad. You'll love this episode. Trust me. It might be an entire season.

And there are billions of actors besides me. Billions of daily and nightly episodes, all fresh content each time. It is all so backward and so ill-advised it is hilarious. Do not underestimate the value of slipping on a banana peel. Let's introduce dinosaurs. Viola! Another kid's show. Let's bring them into current day. Let's give these creatures a taste for human flesh. Zombie dinosaurs! Yes, great idea! You're hired.

Let's experiment with earth processes. Here's an interesting tweak of an idea. What if we do this to evolution? Along come humans. Sex and drugs and rock and roll. There's something for everyone. *Earth: The Freak Show Circus*. That should be my show's name. As long as I am not the only circus freak.

My Whore Went Homeless

She was a long, tall drink of chocolate milk. Sexy skin, firm ass and tits, long tan legs, and extremely capable in bed. I always felt great afterwards with her. But she hated her life. She loved her kids. She loved me. She hated stripping and being pimped. She was an actress. New on the scene. Very talented. She could make you cry or laugh as you came. She was a rollercoaster of emotion. In a dramatic series about prostitutes. It was her first real gig. She made bank, but she worked for it. And the show's writers put her through her paces. I knew she was an actress the moment I saw her at Starbucks. We could never speak of it though. She knew I was a star. We could only speak of things we had done in our present lives on earth. That's in our contracts. We have full nondisclosure clauses that include all personal information. She was educated and 39 years of age. She stripped at a mixed club downtown.

Then one night her landlord went crazy and threw her out. He was a crack head. He wanted pussy and she wouldn't give him any. Reality shows collide. His was about an aberrant asshole drug addict. She loved me. I know. He tossed her shit on the street. She called me. She has three kids from a slightly saner time in her life, her first marriage. Her boy was strong and handsome. The girls smart. That was all she had. And me.

But I had a house full of impossible crazies, not a place for children. I put her up in a weekly hotel room, all four of them in one room. It was the best I could do. I told her she had to pay next week's rent. I live on a limited budget. Also, a contract item. She could not make the rent. And they all went on the streets. A twelve year old girl, a fourteen year old girl, and a sixteen year old man. And her.

Her phone ran out of minutes. Last thing she told me was to meet her at the corner of 6th and Palm at five pm. I waited three hours. It was well past dusk. The cops were beginning to cruise me. I needed to get over the bridge. So I left.

All her online accounts were deleted when I got home. Facebook, Twitter, Instagram, dating sites, everything. All her information wiped out in probably less time than I had waited. I even checked her Ancestry.com account, which, of course, was made up to begin with. I thought maybe she got pulled from the show. She might have confessed something to someone in a desperate moment. That is a huge no-no. On earth, everything the acting guild conducts, regardless of actor or Network card, or even a seed, is fully confidential. You can't tell anyone anything.

It will get you pulled from the show, or worse left behind in poverty. You can get court marshaled, if you are in that position, which I am, or you can simply be executed. If you are an android or other robotic machine, someone might throw your kill switch. Some Networks kill and the shell of the actor remains intact, but the person is essentially dead. I am about to retire, so this is my confession. I got the okay from higher-up. I loved this gal. She knew how to please me. And I took the best care of her I could. And she was funny, witty, a good sense of humor and fair play. She was caring. A very nice woman trapped in a show that she was not ready for.

She appeared on the set one day and an unscrupulous Producer turned her out and got her hooked on drugs. It was a casting couch deal. He pimped her to a porn show at a competing Network. Sold her contract outright. He had a wife and kids. She could cause trouble. I had to do some digging to find that much out. It is not easy to get such information, even on the universal Internet.

She told me how she escaped from the skin flick. They were drugging her up, shooting her up with some cheap shit and piling the Molly McBenders into her. Her head was constantly swimming. She ran. Early one morning. She had nowhere to go. She got on a Greyhound and rode it as far as she could with the forty-four dollars she had. She got off and was on the streets, but she was free. This was before she got married. She met an old Christian couple. They let her sleep it off and fed her, and they helped her get straight. Then she had to run from them. Her life, her story, her job, her show, her mission was to go. That was the name of the show I found out. *Going*. She cursed herself for becoming an actress.

I never heard from her again.

Stephen Covey of the F.B.I. Claims Your "Paymeant" to Citibank is $12 Million Overdue

Africans in Africa and in America must think Americans are dumb as shit. A lot of people do, and while we are getting dumber, and we really are dumb as shit now, we are not quite to *Idiocracy* levels yet. "Go away, bating!" Plus, it's happening around this entire little rock. Many Americans think Africans are dumb as shit. And that they smell bad or wear too much cologne. And why wouldn't we? Don't they know I already paid $12 million to Citibank? I wish Lagos, Nigeria would just lose my phone number and email address. I don't see why I keep getting the same email. It doesn't even say second notice. Most of my bills say second or final notice.

True, America has not tended to its educational system in decades. I know. I teach. At a college where higher math is Algebra. But we are not all that gullible. And I am very sorry that King Niwatumba passed away, but his daughter did not exactly have three and half million in gold bars for me like she claimed. And Stephen Covey quit the F.B.I. years ago. Now who is the big dummy? Don't they know kidnapping white women is where the money is now? A family can even get kidnapping insurance. One of my students informed me of this. They keep it quiet, don't involve the police, and three out of ten times the insurance company gets your wife back. If that's what you want.

"Honey, we are going big game hunting in the African savannas. Put on your best heels. I want you to look good. The guides will meet us at the hotel after we sign some papers. Okay, dear?"

And I am not even from America originally on this planet. I grew up in Africa many millennia ago. It was a lovely spot, but I no longer have most of those memories. The savannas, the falls, everything was so clean and green. A great place to roam. Now it is kind of lean and mean. I haven't been back in this life, but I kind of miss my first home on earth. I wonder if I am still on the "no-fly" list. The motherland of motherlands is beckoning.

Camspeak

"I just saved fifteen percent on my car insurance, Cam." It was a female's very sensual voice. I could tell it was coming from a long way off. The beam was a low tone and strong and hard to recognize. I can sometimes interrupt the transmissions, which means I am higher ranking personnel in the universe. There is a definite ladder, corporate, military, civilian, crew, and otherwise. My show is live and real time everywhere in the universe. I am privy this to information and have been since I was about two years old on earth. My show really launched into its current grandeur when I was an adolescent, and we have held our position as the number one broadcast from earth all this time. That is forty years earth time. Earth is where time goes the slowest in the universe. There are a couple other rocks that fit this scenario, but they are not inhabited by sentient life.

The female "caller", I identify those who beam in as such, told me that the concept of the multi-verse is about to come to fruition in the scientific community on earth. As per my contract, I am trapped in an earth awareness and intellectual state for the most part, and it is my job upon realizing who I am to make my show very interesting. I was Hemingway, "Pistol" Pete Maravic, Houdini, John Cheever, Truman Capote, and others in concurrent or previous forms historically.

One of the rules of alien broadcasts, a common rule, is that the actors are trapped in their native awareness until they experience their own personal awakening. The caller provided useful import to me. The multi-verse is an actual physical, cosmological concept, and an actual, existent structure inside of all of the multi-verse structures that some around the hemisphere have known about for some time. A great many, I assume.

I am broadcast to so many lands I cannot even properly conceive of them all. And I had no idea the proof was in the pudding and about to be discovered in great array, especially that this discovery was imminent here on earth. The theoretical scientists on the Astronomy shows on the local set are about to prove its existence. I heard one of them or a small group of scientists has a verifiable equation or theorem or proof that is correct. I am not a scientist. The proof defines the existence in mathematical and symbolic form of the multi-verse. One or two of them are notable authors here on the local set, concerning what is known from an earth perspective of the cosmos.

I am thrilled. That means my show is going to a much larger audience than even I had imagined. I am in for an even bigger dip into the retirement fund. Rebecca loves knowing this as well. We speak daily, if we are able. Rebecca can shop. And her sidekick, Meg Darling, is our gal pal from another very important house. I chose both of them as my cohorts, and they chose me back, and this occurred again at some recent point in earth history for us, and we cemented our bonds this time.

Rebecca and my kids are getting a bump up in the academies they attend. They will be among the finest known. And it may mean they have to admit me to the ranks of the Producers after all, because I'll have more money than any of them. In which case, I may not retire. Except maybe one or two Producers from my Network, I am the richest man in the jar. I use the term "man" loosely. Anthropomorphizing. The" jar" is the known territory to include what is out there that is known to be out there, even if uncharted, and what is unknown to be out there. Because it's there too.

Rebecca and I can park our next vacation home anywhere inside the jar. The jar is the multi-verse, which contains an infinite number of universes, some real, some imaginary, some unreal, some alternative or parallel, some mostly dark matter, some matter, some anti-matter. And there could be others of which I am still unaware. Earth awareness is not great. My theory, which I'll work on in retirement is that there is an infinite number of multi-verses. I have seen the doors to them. I know I can go through and get back, but I don't know at what point I'll be able. Certainly not from earth. It won't be allowed. Or maybe so, but I prefer to never come back to this ghetto.

The big boys at the corporate headquarters of my Network sprung for some very expensive equipment to pull this off. The concept of the multi-verse was actually a brainstorm of someone at my Network. He worked on it his whole life. I am not certain if he is an immortal, but probably; however, there are fewer of us than most think. The multi-verse the corporate suits set into action is along evolutionary lines because evolution is merely a process that tweaks and experiments with itself constantly, and by so doing on the part of my Network hotshots, no one will ever figure out the proper theorems. The design, patent, prototype are priceless. The existent form is even more valuable. Every sponsor's dream, and my Network pulled it off.

And the multi-verse includes a method of time rippling. That closes the door on the competition. I think it works like a reset point on a computer, but few have access to it or all the data. It is a jealously guarded secret and very hush-hush. They know I am checking out soon, so

I got the okay to break the word. This is my low key way of announcing this important find. Only some life forms can use the information and processes effectively and safely. This also slams the door on the competition. Its use is geared to my race of people, and we are a very old race of individuals, from outside all the jars originally at a beginning point.

My earthling self, I can run along time concurrencies, past, present, future, as well as astral project, which has a real time feature involved, and I can also shift time, time slot, and I can slide time, but even I have not figured out time rippling yet. I got so good at these techniques, I can cross a street and be on another planet. I even know how to go through a black hole device, not an actual black hole yet though. I can come out the other side through the worm hole at the end, which is a great way to elude the police or other nefarious nasty types looking for me, and I have gotten so good at this I can put the device, which has no physical properties, in any entrance, door, gate, or opening one would pass through, even say an arch or column, but I have not tried with an actual black hole. Black holes pulverize matter so frequently that nothing comes out in its original form. But time rippling intrigues me. I will learn this approach. Something to do with the grand kids in my old age.

"Marvelous," I said. "Do you know what a car is, my dear?" I am protecting the caller to my show. It is subterfuge. Everyone is trying to trace her transmission. I am well aware it's because of the distance. The farther away from earth a beam is that's received, the more valuable the information is considered. When a competitor traces a caller, he or she can gain insight into the technology and level of science and creative prowess in the area, thus he might be able to steal something. The shows that are scripted have the writers and their staffs do this all the time.

"Sure, I enjoy your show all the time. The cars look like great fun." She picks up immediately that I am being discreet and trying to avoid any personal encumbrances for her. It is my duty as a well-rounded host.

"Then you have never been in a three car pile-up or had a blowout on a bridge in the soaking rain. Where do you hail from, hotness?" I had to get a little flirt on. I had gotten in the habit too of inquiring where my voices came from. The stock answer was the Pleaides, but sometimes they told the truth.

"The Northeast Quadrant, Cam. Home of the Super Burger." Just by stating the word "quadrant", when the current, more preferred usage is now elliptical, at least on earth, she is giving away to some that she is in a past point in time, or comes from a very distant past life, and plenty realize their attempted search of her address or quadrant is futile. She knows this as well. She has fully protected herself. The competition can be vicious. Espionage is a well known trait and activity around the greater hemisphere. Even considered by some a time-honored tradition.

"Wow. I am impressed. I love it out there."She was making a joke about the super burger. It wasn't funny to me, but by the way she chortled I assumed she thought it was. Or perhaps it was a hidden message buried in the context of what she said to me. The Northeast Quadrant is a very sophisticated part of the universe. "I am flattered," I said. "Only been the one time though. You are on the other side of the universe from me. Earth is on the cusp of the northwest and southwest quadrants."

"I know. We learn that in second form geography as infants. The Milky Way is a barred spiral galaxy. You are too funny. A bunch of my friends are here."

"Hey Cam!" A chorus of lovelies breaks out.

"Hello! So what do you eat in the Northeast Quadrant? I am hungry. A burger sounds good."

"I am not supposed to say. You know the rules. They are going to cut me off for this, but we have what you would call trees everywhere that are full of edible vegetation. But we never get hungry, so we don't really eat ever. The trees are for visitors. We like visitors. My time is up, Cam. Come visit. I love you!"

"Wow! That was warm," I said aloud. The communications are for the most part what one might consider telepathic, though many are of an energetic quality altogether, and have nothing to do with telepathy, more like a beam or teletransmissive or telekinetic stream. Some are pure energy. These cannot yet be harnessed or measured on earth. Some life forms use devices. I have never needed one though. "I'll come as soon as I can catch a transport, or maybe I can astral project. Let me see Rebecca and the kids first, and then I'll come for sure. Bye, ladies."

Always nice to have a destination in mind. I like it out there, but it is not a slow pace. The denizens are referred to as Goddesses. The entire quadrant is inhabited solely by what one might describe as females. They look every bit the part of Goddesses when they are inclined to take a form. It's lovely there.

But I was thinking with my earthbound self. I am on my home planet as well. I had bi-located, but it had become a bit of a disconnect. Sometimes I wasn't really sure I had made it home. I know I have. It is for my own personal safety, but rarely am I able to see or talk to myself in my other form. I can go to the Northeast Quadrant any time. The woman with the sexy voice could still hear me, of course. Certain very capable fans of mine can hear every inch of my thoughts. I had to speak aloud for some others to understand. Others still, I must use a device, but an ordinary cell phone or television will do. It is tricky talking to my fans aloud in public spaces or with someone around. I have to pretend I am on the phone. They will even tell me to pick up my phone to avert suspicion.

The transmitters on the young lovely's planet had been shut down, but not the receiver. She told me she was aware they would be. It goes against the rules of the providers that I or most other actors be given specific types of information. The receivers are always up. The cable company or Internet providers, relative terms to an earth approximate understanding, have that in the contract, I am sure. 24/7. That's an earth expression, of course. But my fans understand mostly. They have a good sense of earth time and physical laws and properties. Mainly it comes from watching my show. Otherwise, no one would care about earth really. So many have watched my shows for eons. Since the dawn of many of their own creations. In a sense, many of my fans grew up with me. The Network likes to build in generational viewing.

They are advanced forms in the Northeast Quadrant. I was there during a laborers' strike a long time ago. It was kind of messy. A lot of ice Goddesses live in this quadrant. They all think with one central mind, so they all know what the other is doing every moment of the day and night. Day and night are earth notions as well. We have only the one sun on earth. I would assume there is a terrific lack of privacy, but as they are warriors primarily, the ice Goddesses, no one is going to sneak attack them, if they can all see through each other's eyes and hear each other's thoughts. They are a bunch of very beautiful and powerful women. No one to trifle with. I love them. I have a tremendous following among them.

They can assume human form. And it is always as a woman as far as I know. I see them on earth from time to time. I am anthropomorphizing a tad. The ice Goddesses are gorgeous as sin. Sexy, sexy too. Rebecca might allow me to take a holiday that way. She can be very understanding about things of this nature. It is not such a sensitive detail for us. I never fail to return home to Rebecca and Meg and our kids.

I would go in the summer. Their winters (once again an earth notion as some parts of the universe have only the one season, or nothing relative to a season on earth at all) are brutally cold. They have buildings and mountains built of ice and glass. Palatial houses too. The views are fabulous. And clean fiords that you can swim in, if you like near freezing water, which I do. We skinny dipped the time I was there in a mountain lake, and the temperature of the water was probably about 45 degrees Fahrenheit. They had heated it up for me. And then we hit the sauna and made love all afternoon.

But I can't go at present. I have other things going on at the moment. I am writing a language. For posterior. (Camspeak).

So I just introduced one facet of Camspeak. Not much of a segway into this particular vignette, but Camspeak is similar to Newspeak of the Orwellian hellish variety as depicted in Orwell's classic novel *1984*. I believe I was George Orwell in a concurrent earth form, but at a time before I was born as myself now, Cam. But Camspeak is not meant to have the same limiting effects. In fact, quite the opposite. And it is not about control, but fun rather.

In Newspeak, say for instance, the concept is sad, and the polar opposite in Newspeak would be unsad. Newspeak is designed so the individual who learns it cannot envision and has no concept of the antonym or antipodes in denotation or connotation of a word.

If you take my example of unsad, someone who has grown up speaking Newspeak would not know the word happy, and therefore have no concept of what happy means or feels like. Primarily, this lends to control issues. It would not exist in the language, hence in reality either. It all gets back to Sapir-Whorf and their hypothesis that if you have language for something, it then exists, and vice-versa, I suppose. If you can't verbalize it, according to Sapir-Whorf, it doesn't exist. I may be extrapolating.

Camspeak emphasizes what is good and is one way to create. I like to create harmony and fun, but not always together. They are distinct concepts and emotions. Camspeak is most likely a children's language, which suits me fine. In my own race of alien I am comparable to an eight year old on earth, in a relative point of view, of course.

Another example. Camspeak is basically the polar opposite of Newspeak in a way. If something is funny, or if it is unfunny, the individual would not have a concept for something that is not funny. In turn, hopefully the person would go through life seeing great mirth in everything. It could be kind of "idiotizing" or retarding in this case. Most of life on earth is tragic; however, there are great comic moments in tragedy. I am still working on the fundamentals and a prototype of the language. It is rather complex. Conditionals are giving me problems. How should something be, if it simply cannot be at all?

There is another less formal side to Camspeak too. It is saying inane things meant to spark conversation. I was in the kitchen cutting up some tomatoes. Mr. Bunion, my roommate on the hospital crew, comes up to me and says, "what are you going to put on those?"

I say, "cream cheese." And then I take a bottle of olive oil and drizzle the bowl of tomatoes with it. I proceed to sit down at the table and eat my tomatoes.

Mr. Bunion says, "what about the cream cheese, Cam?"

"Are we out of cream cheese?"

"You said you were going to put cream cheese on the tomatoes."

"I know."

"That's olive oil." At this point the plumber usually chimes in with, "this is the worst conversation I have ever heard." He's known for that line on set, even though none of my roommates have their actor's card. The giggles I hear do not escape me often.

"Yes," I say. "The heat is certainly extenuating today." As in an extenuating or mitigating circumstance. Mr. Bunion and the plumber never quite know if I am playing or not. They are both very bright, so they call me an idiot and leave it at that. But I had my fun. Seems a little nerdish to me, but nerds know how to have fun. They just don't play well together or usually with others. I have always been a little bookish.

So here's a further example of Camspeak in action. Mr. Bunion and I were driving back from the ghetto Wal-Mart. No terrific flashes of light this time. But he saw a woman, in her mid-twenties apparently, an attractive, pleasing shape, who looked like she was going to try and cross the busy street. Then he said, "oh, my! That semi flattened her." There was no laughter in my head, so I assume it was off-peak hours for the show. The jocularity and ensuing screams of pleasure would have deafened me momentarily otherwise. I had seen the same woman too. She looked very tentative like she was not used to crossing in traffic.

"She was a Presbyterian," I said. (Camspeak). Mild chuckles. My audience must be out to dinner, I gather.

"How do you know that?"

"She was on foot."

"You are thinking of Mormons, and they ride bicycles," Mr. Bunion said. "Oh, you mean pedestrian."

"Quite so. Here comes the ambulatory," I said. (Camspeak).

"You mean, ambulance," Mr. Bunion said.

"Definitively," I said.

I know Camspeak is ahead of its time. The historians will prove this point. And if something is historical, how is something else, or its obverse, unhistorical? As in, it is happening now, or simply of no consequence. It is historical, and therefore significant, but it is not at the same moment of realization. Perhaps both are correct. That may be for the historians to decide as well. As soon as they are born. And can someone be unborn? Or unpregnant? Or undead? I suppose so. It's tricky. So tricky.

The CIA Murdered Me

Red and black, friend of Jack. Black and red, you're dead. The CIA was up to its old tricks. Was that a Corn snake or a Coral snake? There's one sure way to find out. Let it bite you and see if you die. It wasn't really a snake. A friend told me about his trip to Peru. There was a snake in the mission compound. Poisonous snakes have neurotoxin. Someone had injected me with neurotoxin again. Probably in my sleep as I said. They keep coming and going from my house. And sometimes they stick me with needles. This time it might kill me.

It might have been the KGB. Always with the plausible deniability. Reagan learned that. I was involved with causing some very high level scientists from Moscow to defect to the U.S. Don't ask me what I did. I am not sure. I guess they took my advice. Better hookers and bigger apartments stateside. The scientists touched their plane down somewhere, fueled up, lost their original crew and pilot, and flew straight to New York.

So I can't really say it was the CIA for sure, but I received a very slow acting neurotoxin that hides in the body and cannot be detected. It mirrors Multiple Sclerosis and eventually will kill me. Luckily, I can pop into the future and cure myself.

Maybe they did me a favor. Whoever it was. I have to shed this body anyway perhaps. But I may not have to. Lately, the Network employees have been saying they can just age regress my body. I told them I want to be as my twenty-nine year old self here on earth. I was a body sculptor then. Who needs eternal youth and beauty. I say wear it out. Get a new one or hit the reset switch. If cellular degeneration is a thing, cellular regeneration must be too.

I am immortal, so a little poison is not going to do much, but my knees and back sure hurt like hell. If it was the CIA, they are a bunch of ungrateful bastards. I have helped them plenty, but they are such a pack of pussies. They are always scared when someone knows something. The old line understood and knew how to manage me. Every one of them was murdered, I think. Now it is all gangsta thug punks. Dumb fucks with an attitude.

Funny thing about this is my dad died the same way. My earth dad. He was basically a putz. He sold me into slavery when I was two. He worked for the same douches. They were obligated to take care of me, and they did to an extent. They poisoned him as well. He had CIA and KGB connections. No one was ever certain what side of the fence he was on.

40

Some said he was a good man; others said he should have been shot for treason.

He rid the U.S. Embassy in Moscow of listening devices back in the very early 80's. The Russian contractors had built them into the walls, but my earth father found every last one of them, and disconnected them right under the Russians' noses. Nerves of steel. Then he flew home and retired from the CIA. Then almost immediately after, he got sick and had a lingering, painful death. He always said, "if they are gonna get ya, they are gonna get ya."

He was a very paranoid man, but liberated in a sense too, and shrewd, because they did get him and he understood what had happened. He was very much the patriot, I think. I doubt he was an earthling. I saw him five times my whole life, and other than the time he kidnapped me and took me to Japan, which is a country I dearly love, he and I were mostly at odds with each other our entire lives.

Those were peak seasons in the Cold War. He was good. A good spy. I'll give him that. He once, near his death, apologized for getting me into the mess he did, but he never disclosed a thing to me. I figured it all out, and the Network let me know several jewels of information that he had done to me. The Russians were on to him, and he forged my name on the flight papers as he made a quick exit, so it looked like I had been in Moscow with him and assisted, but I have never been to Moscow.

I had a mission before America was even in existence. Any country for that matter. It didn't come about until I was born an American, but part of my show included saving this lonely, desolate rock known as earth. And the ratings were so high, they just basically rewrote the scenarios, so I did it over and over. One reason earth history repeats itself. Basically every reality television show has only the one script. But soon I am released from my acting indentured servitude. I saved this entire piece of shit planet at least seven times from complete annihilation at the hands of alien marauders, or at least abject poverty and enslavement for its residents. And I don't even like this planet. It has also grown so ugly to me.

I was always a lot older than my dad. And more capable. When I was born as his son, he was a mere baby in comparison. Not even a vision of bedroom eyes in a woman's dream. If he stemmed from the Pleiades originally, which I believe he did, it would mean that he might have been

41

ten to twenty thousand years old, if that. A true infant with an infant's understanding of so much.

I was on earth at least five million years before he got here. I was the original hominid, Lucy. I was at a point a hermaphrodite. I might have been his grandfather's grandfather ad infinitum. I have a lot of history with earth and much more way beyond. I would not claim him in my family anyway. Rebecca and Meg deserve top flight in-laws. My real father is very cool. More powerful and engaging than I am. Plus, he dotes on his son.

I was never born on the Pleaides. It is a nasty overpopulated place, and the water especially is not fit to drink. They shot a show on location there about me called *The Pleaidean Guy*. It was set on earth contemporary time and the man who played me was acting the part of an earthling that went around claiming he was a Pleaidean. On earth. He gets locked up, thrown in the psychiatric jails called hospitals, depressing stuff, but funny to them. Why anyone would claim he or she was Pleaidean is beyond me.

It made some serious bank too, until the director got burned up completely in full view of the cast right on set one day in a freak accident, and everyone assumed it was an omen. The Pleaideans are a very religious race usually. Personally, I give a rat's ass about any of it. Religion or some dead hack of a director. I'll get my share of the royalties. I am under contract. They can't misappropriate my name. It was a small house with limited reach that wrote and broadcast the show, and the ones who ran it thought no one would find out, but obviously someone did. Freak accidents don't just happen on the Pleaides. Which planet in the constellation it was, I am not sure. My Network knows.

The spy game is a rough one so often. Interstellar spies are hard to catch. The ones that they do know of usually get murdered. I knew a nice portly fellow that bent over to pick up a handkerchief he had dropped on the curbside, and got it in the ass end with the poison tip of an umbrella. That one was curare. They wanted to make sure he didn't talk. He died before I could get help. He and I were in Greece, I think. I knew he was a spy, but he seemed happy and carefree enough. Something big must have happened. They don't usually kill you right away.

Plausible deniability. As I said. And the CIA and other law enforcement and intelligence types are just now discovering how many true aliens, extraterrestrials, there are here on earth. They watch their steps a little more closely now.

This guy that got the curare butt shot and I were waiting outside and were about to join my father on a rare occasion for me inside a hotel to have dinner, and he was definitely murdered. His heart didn't stop naturally like the coroner stated in his report. I saw this happen. Right in front of me. I was maybe nine years old. I had to lie to the police. His mistress was distraught. Whatcha gonna do? Live till you die, and go out and dance a little and have a few drinks, breaks some plates on the floor, and sing in the shower, if the spirit moves you. I have a ride home. I don't worry about anything. The rest of earth's population should be very concerned. Especially once I am gone. I ain't never no ways coming back. Another of my code names is Heart Attack. I go out with guns blazing till my heart blows up. It did once already. I never even went inside the ER. Next time there won't be time. I am fine with it.

LRAD and the CIA's Thought Microphones

Project Blue Beam. I worked on this for the U.S. government and the U.S. Armed Forces. It was a joint venture with the CIA. It is a very powerful weapon. It will creep up on you and destroy you in moments...all lickety split like. You'll never know what hit you. And you'll be dead as a doornail. And your crew or platoon or ship. When I get my new body, my family will have to change my neural net. I will no longer be susceptible then. French fries to us. As in small potatoes. We are mostly a pack of scientists. And I might come back and destroy the earth. I am not into enslaving mankind. I would rather eradicate it. A bunch of peasants in my considered opinion. I save them and this is how I get repaid. I like women and money and whiskey. That's about it. Let the cockroaches take over. It's fitting.

Project Blue Beam is a digitized signal. I helped the CIA and the military pinpoint it so precisely, people think the signals are their own thoughts.

LRAD. Long Range Acoustical Device. It started out on U.S. carriers as a way to tell smaller boats to get out of the way. It essentially was a warning device. The Captain or yeoman of the carrier could speak into the device and hit his voice very close to the ears of the others on nearby

43

ships. Only the others, typically foreign sailors, thought they were hearing the voice of God. Or the Devil. They would become very scared and freak out.

So, the CIA got involved and figured out a way to weaponize LRAD. They used it on me, and I helped them pinpoint the beam with such accuracy, now it appears to come from inside your head. So, now LRAD seems like it is your own thought. So when you hear the voice of God, you actually are hearing someone with that code name. God is code for a very high ranking CIA player. Satan is God's number one man. Only I know much better, but most can't tell the difference from their own thoughts. It is so precisely attuned. If they need to, they can brain spat you and hook it up so it appears as a synaptic response. All it takes is a wide area MRI to download the information necessary. It got the name Project Blue Beam and a bunch of Air Force officers developed it for the military. It is very low-tech too, surprisingly. Which makes it more efficient, as we all know the fewer working parts, the less likely something will break down.

They used LRAD the last time in Iraq. The Iraqi soldiers were sure they were hearing the devil's own voice. It can paralyze you with fear. Freeze you in your tracks. And then when the effects wear off, you go home, get good and liquored up, and jump off a building. And a buddy of mine that was formerly Air Force told me they can split the sin wave now, so they can send the thoughts anywhere and in all directions. It's like Wi-Fi on acid and steroids. Only it is actually someone speaking into a microphone. It is pretty paranoia making shit. And they can use it on anyone.

I honestly did not know the CIA and the military would weaponize it. They made it seem like a game to me. I really am a child. Comparatively, outside the jar I am about eight years old. All the while they had me blasted on hallucinogens. They use it against me constantly now, but they cannot penetrate my head with it. They even torture my cat with it. But I know when something is external and when something is internal. Most don't or can't tell, especially if they are new to this technology. It is like a whisper on the waves. A rustling of leaves on the tree. God's voice. A dream. A hallucination. I have an earthling's body, but my very illustrious family protects me from their shit. I wish I had never worked with the CIA. They have no sense of loyalty or compassion to anyone or anything, not the president, not the government, not the

44

military, not even themselves. They are a bunch of dangerous boys and girls with high-tech toys. Or low-tech in the case of LRAD.

The Swiss Clock

People speculate on the beginning of the world, meaning earth, the universe and stars, and everything in them. They speculate endlessly. Especially here on earth. As I have mentioned many times, I am immortal. I go back before the earth was ever a planet. Thirteen or fourteen billion years is a blink of the eye to me. Earth started as a fantasy. It was actually a twinkling in a very gifted set designer's mind, and became a real feather in his cap among many, but seriously went awry.

I don't go back as far as the beginning of the all, but I am known as everything. I stem from all. All was the beginning. I can't remember that far back. I might not stick around for the next creation too long. Where I go is back into the forward time: the future. The creation is already in progress. It is the ninth one I know of. Some get there, but most don't. I have been around for eight creations, and I know I go to the ninth, but not for long. I go outside of everything back to all. It seems very simplistic, but these are true, factual terms. There is no other relevant way to define these matters.

When you are talking about earth that is a lot of history with the planet, about fourteen billion years (earth time). This is a much shorter or much longer time depending on where you live in the universe, but for our sakes, we'll keep it as earth time, because that is where I seem to be stuck again. I have lived on earth about five million of its fourteen billion years.

Unfortunately, however, I have lost touch with Rebecca and Meg Darling and the girls again, except by voice and thought, so I am left to assume there is a time limit to bi-location, meaning I could only do it for a specified period of time. I honestly did not know that. I know there is a time limit to shifting, or as some know it to be called time shifting or sliding. Astral projection is for an even shorter time. Astral projection might be just a night's sleep for me. Rippling is another matter. I have not yet learned how to ripple time. I will though. We go beyond time travel in the next universe. It is all about the rippling effect, which, in essence, brings everything to you. You can remain on the couch. And it is not virtual. It is real. All the physical laws of nature still apply, depending on one's location, of course.

So I was talking about earth and the universe. The entire universe goes back, I think, if you subscribe to the Big Bang Theory, about fourteen to eighteen billion years. Correct me, if I am wrong. Or don't. I haven't brushed up on my physics or astronomy in a while. We know very little of any certainty on earth. Our absolute truths amount to the sun rises in the east and sets in the west. Gravity is still a theory on earth. So is evolution. We are quite backward here.

The earth and the Milky Way, which is a small galaxy within the Virgo Super Cluster, have been in physical form in the universe much of this time, but perhaps not all of this time. The fourteen billion years or so. Earth years again. Pardon me. I have been here so long now, and the passage of time here is so important on this planet, it is the only true measurement I know now. I did start measuring distance again in parsecs, which was easy as soon as I knew to again. Earth is kind of a prison and kind of an experimental television set. There are the constant erasure of memories and the fiddling with the neural net of earthlings as constant variables, for lack of a better term.

But the creature known as God on earth actually did create earth, but he is not what we know from the bible. The bible is a story. He is not the man behind the code name either that works for the CIA. The bible is a clever analogy, like an epic poem, one that many people on earth have taken at face value. The true origin is unknown. It could have been a doctoral thesis. Or a play. Or originally rhymed couplets. Same with the Koran, the Talmud, the Gita, etc., etc. Merely doctrine and stories.

All of an earthly nature. God was not an author, and, of course, he is not known as God elsewhere. I've met the man one time. When I met him, he went by the name Brian. My Producer introduced me to him. Brian has a very cool lab. He's charming enough, an exquisite engineer, a better architect, has great attention for detail, and worked for a production company that wanted to launch a new series about the evolution of a planet and solar system and the human race. He is known to be a patient gentleman.

The viewers of the original broadcast are all either dead now or have run and hidden in terror. The story was a great one till man evolved. But that left room for many comedies of a tragic sort. And yes, man evolved. Engineering tool. Set the mechanism and take five. Swiss clock. Swiss clocks keep perfect time, but if you watch one, it will drive you insane. So, it is kind of funny on my show when someone prays to God. My fans love it. Brian took off his headset billions of years ago. He was, before he retired, or went on to other projects, an architect, a set designer, and craftsman.

He did this before man on earth existed. And my viewers find it hysterical when someone quotes the bible. Of course, it is usually misquoted. Even funnier. And the laws we pass on this planet. C-Span is a very popular Network around the sphere. It's hilarious. Most of earth is a big farce. It went from science program to a children's story to a very campy horror/reality show.

So here's the funny notion. If you are from earth, the creationists and the evolutionists are both right. Their respective timetables are a bit off, however. Earth was very fertile ground in concept and reality. It was intended to make money. What would you do if you were making tons of money selling your shows and products to an adoring and growing public? You would keep making shows and selling products. That is essentially what Brian's production company did. He is extremely well known in the industry. I guess he sort of is a God. (Earth anthropomorphizing).

Here is what I know for certain. Shithead, my cat, is curling up at my feet, I have a good book in front of me, a full belly, and nowhere to be for the next couple of days. It's what you make it. I might not even be certain of this. It could simply all be allusion or an illusion or some child pulling my strings with a new video game he received by interstellar parcel. Or a computer program ala the Matrix that went horribly wrong, and at any rate...we are all going to die! I stole that, but it's true. I think. But not me. Or maybe none of us. I don't know now. Wait, there it is again. I've got it. Oops, I forgot!

My Queen is on earth!

I met Rebecca. Again. In the flesh. At my house this time. I had seen her once before in an alien hospital for sex offenders not on earth (because there are such things on earth). Or was it for the criminally insane? She and I were captives there. It was on location during my last season before my contract was picked up again for the final last season, the end of my show. It might have been on Calderon Three. They might have tried to commit me then as well. My earth brother tried in the final season of my show. He failed. I do not understand the technical aspects of alien commitments. Or Pleaidean law for that matter. I don't understand alien medical practices. The ones perpetrated on earth are a sham and a disgrace.

When my brother tried in one of my near-to-final episodes in 2016 A.D. (earth time appreciation) to commit me, it never went in front a judge. It was 2016 on earth, but it was simultaneously a point in a future reality the second time I was to be committed and locked up. I had harmed no one. I had merely a second degree misdemeanor on record then from trespassing against a structure. I was set up. I heard the screams of a woman I knew. She was a neighbor of mine. A nice young lady. So I tried to assist and was arrested. As if this constituted grounds for commitment. My earth brother lost his place then and there by his actions by his own hands for all time. Our dad had already. He made it out, but they will hunt him, and I will look the other way.

Once again, it might not have been on earth as I understood earth to be. I really did not understand why I was being held in the psychiatric prison. I was not informed there was a commitment procedure (an ex-parte action) against me, but, as I said, it had not been in front of a judge, nor did it ever go in front of a judge. But tell that to an idiot hospital staff. They kept me there despite my protests, and beat me up twice. Nine men working at the hospital jumped me because they had angered me severely and would not release me, and I kept spitting on their dayroom window, so they forced me to one knee and broke my shoulder. At present this is my most unforgettable memory of my latest round of freedom fighting. It was not really broken, merely badly sprained, but permanently dislocated.

I heard they were all executed before I awoke the next day. Members of the opposing Network. Perhaps they had duped my earth brother, or paid him, or he worked against me. I knew him not well as any brother of mine. The nine demons from Hell looked funny the next morning. Like caricatures of themselves. They looked like they had not showered or eaten or slept. All nine of them. I could tell they had died.

I laughed at them the following day and called them pussies. Nine large hospital orderlies and they could force me, starved-out again, to one knee only. They will serve in Hell appropriately forever. My Hell that I give, not theirs. And the God they don't wish to pray to. His is the Lake of Fire. Mine is known as Fire Island. Resistance is futile! A bunch of Nazis. All they ever were.

But onto a much more important matter. This time that I saw Rebecca, I was not horribly starved out like before as when I saw her in the alien mental hospital. Aliens love to mess with the food staples on earth and other supplies for earthlings. They trap them in their zoos and prisons. Some use them for target practice. They enslave them in their own hells. I have liberated them all across the universe. One of the more socially redeeming points of my show. Plus, it makes for great viewership.

The more clandestine aliens produce horrific food additives as well on earth as a result of alien research, and medications, poison the jet stream, use varying intensity of flashes of light from interstellar television beamed from their Networks, cell phone transmissions from satellites managed by ET's, and these components further layer down the earth population for bondage and internment. I gave up on earth, and my show closes up soon, and I and my company leave here never to return. Earth grew a nastier and nastier pustule of locale. Once a garden spot, a hidden gem, but no more.

Rebecca and I got the chance to speak the second time we met. We had never spoken face-to-face before. We spoke by my swimming pool as I grilled steaks and kielbasa in my old house that was foreclosed eventually upon by alien mortgage brokers. We are not married yet, although she is my Queen (my top Queen of seven ladies), and we live together already in the future and all of us as well outside the jar. We are already there. What is left on earth is our refuse. Our shells that run out of energy and keel over and die.

I am simultaneously an eight year old and a twenty-nine year old in an earth understanding, and I am the same man, and I am the King of the multi-verse. I own outright half of the multi-verse. I enhanced the multi-verse that had come into existence through an evolutionary process and made it my own. They say it is fabulous though I have not seen exactly.

And I had enhanced Rebecca this time around, previous to our meeting the first time in the criminal nut ward. She stood staunchly in my corner as always. As did our friends. Most notably Meg Darling and my brothers Bot1 and Bot2. My significant other labored behind the scenes. The Chosen One waited and observed. We all go up, out, and into the future and then outside the multi-spaces, some know them as hyper-spaces, where space, time, and matter are meaningless concepts. Some know them as inter-dimensional. We are and become again pure energy. And energy is neither created nor destroyed. I am of this family. And I at my sole discretion and approval of my parental energy can bring others into it.

Rebecca was never of earth. I was born on earth approximately twenty-five million years ago, when my latest of shows began, and evolved as Lucy, the original hominid, an australopithecene, at about the five million year mark B.C. A trivial blip in my life. I have been a star a long time prior. But now Rebecca and I are back together again. For good this time. Forever. But not entirely just yet. Not till my consciousness here on earth fully merges with my future selves. Then I am home with my house in the future, and certain ones of us go immediately outside the jar.

I found Rebecca one day through the universal Internet. You know the one that Al Gore created. I chose her to be my accomplice on stage. We are not really fleshly creatures. Neither of us human nor humanoid. Most of this latest creation was human or humanoid. I come from long before. As the lead character in my show, I began as nothing but a seed; however, I am the first and sole existing proof of human evolution on earth. That was a quite a few series ago.

Rebecca and my troops are time-benders and time-shifters in a very basic form, and we can come in and out of different multi-phasic and spatial time and space coordinates in different states of matter and at different levels of energy. My Network is the original Network. We came before it all. There was one other Network near the start, and we have been at war forever. The opposing Network and its subsidiaries have waged an eternal battle that I was sent to barter or solve diplomatically; and as a resulting failure on my part with a peaceful approach, I then became a soldier and fought. I eradicated the existing competition that would not stand down. I did it for the honor of my family, the leading members of the original Network. And myself and my queens and my many wives and my children.

I battled interminably and the other Network's remaining members have recently surrendered, and the war is over, and we, of my house that are left, all go home. Our enemies are trapped on earth and will perish. All of them. I am originally from the House of Nine, and we picked up one more who helped in our struggles, so now we are the House of Ten. But we soon after became the House of Fourteen, and we have one single appointee left to make. God's house is the House of Eight. I was an original member of this house as well. But things for me did not go as planned and I left that company of actors. We, at present the House of Fourteen, are the actors and agents of the multi-verse, and I come from before it all, and we shall reign in our proper places upon arrival with me at my home outside everything that is known and unknown, the jar. We go beyond the sixteen universes. The sixteen houses.

Rebecca, the second time we met, was not announced in any way. To go home and a good woman is all I ever really wanted. I have seven now, and two close male associates, my brothers, that have proved their loyalty to me time and again. My Producer wished I remain on earth one final season. I have known several good women and several good friends, and I chose wisely from the cast and crew who shall come with me. I am in multiple realities and time and space coordinates all at the same time, at the same point of convergence, in the same body, and I have many houses now of fine women from many parts of the various universes, but one main house that leaves the show and comes with me. And now there are more of us outside the jar, waiting on me to retire, merge, and be reborn. The King and Queen await, as they are my father and mother, the return of some and a few new arrivals, my close companions and me.

Less so for Meg Darling, but even for Rebecca there are very obvious reasons not to be with a man like me. Few women truly want a soldier. Meg Darling enjoys that I am a soldier. Meg Darling is my other top queen. It makes her feel safe that I am a soldier. Many women think they do, but often they really don't want a man who fights. But if I were a just a soldier, I might understand being passed up so much and so often. I am from a long line of kings, but I started with nothing. Over and over again, I began with nothing. Earth, the earlier creations, the stars, the jar are all rites of passage. I go beyond them all. Outside of the stars. Outside of the universes. Outside the one true multi-verse. Outside of the known. Outside of the unknown. My troops and I. That is where I and choice few others are from. It is our home.

Rebecca spoke a pleasant hello. She smiled. I died in that moment. I saw myself travel through space. I went home again that instant and have been there ever since. I am safe and so are the others. That is why Rebecca and I and our close friend Meg Darling and the other gals can talk so freely with each other. And there are two Androids that are male, who are brothers of mine, and one other that is female that is my close friend as well. All of us take on a vast array of shapes and forms, and numerous key ones, as the situation dictates.

The screenplay is intensely original and complicated. Only certain parts are scripted. We go undetected to the unsuspecting unless we allow. We are all presently living outside of everything and outside the jar. But we come in periodically and put on our show. We go home and come back to work. The show continues, but it is soon over for us. Soon we go and remain out and become known as the House of Fourteen. But we add another.

It is my show and it does well for all of us, but the scenes get more hellish constantly. The jails, the prisons, the hospitals, the various lock-ups, the demonic cops, the androids, the robots, the drones, the slatterns, the screw balls, the petty tyrants, the assholes on earth...I have had to scour high and low for all my best cast members, and it is finally decided who comes with me at the close of my show. It will be a grand party the night the curtain finally drops for good. Confetti and ticker tape. A cast party to end all cast parties.

The bank was right, meaning we have all profited exceedingly well. A term from an earth girl I knew that committed suicide. I loved her and I was going to propose one evening. She killed herself on a trip to the Catskills she had planned. I had asked her not to go.

The calls kept coming in for the show. Other Networks tried to sabotage it, but I have been a star a long time. A seed learns all the tricks of the trade. I knew well what to expect. The live format was proceeding in a glowing fashion. The cast was happier than I think I had ever seen them. But we were all anxious. It has been a long, grueling final season. We wanted to close out things. The final season was turning out to be a real gut-wrencher and a real show-blower. It was a tough season for me personally and the cast and crew.

We had put together a solid piece of programming everywhere we had gone for quite a long time now. Freedom fighters know no bounds. Even on earth it is a hit. And the technical tools are very challenging to work with on earth. Earth is in the Forbidden Zone, and it is risky to travel here. Very few ever get out, and most die excruciatingly painful deaths in complete destitution and desperation and anonymity. The opposing Networks had followed me in, and the trap was laid. They are all condemned to servitude and death on earth.

We had hit another critical juncture in the show on earth. I was soon to retire. My earth body grew old and disaffected. The Producer wanted me, the other stars, the House of Fourteen as we became known, the show's members, the support cast, the crew, the audience, the sponsors, the advertisers, the marketers, the cable providers, and, of course the Network, which continues on anyway, to go out with one last final big bang for my show. Rebecca and I didn't even know what it would be. She had taken over as Femme Fatale. Meg Darling became Le Petit Anjou. And we have several close friends now. There are several star performers now in my show. We grew into an impressive, unbeatable ensemble production.

Rebecca and Meg Darling: My Two Queens of the Show

Rebecca and Meg Darling. Femme Fatale and Le Petit Anjou. Rebecca and I had been in touch often ever since I created her acting capacities in 2008 A.D. I did not actually create Rebecca. I found her and enhanced her skills in a major way. I coached her perhaps. She was already a star. But I created her star power one might say. She had been a simple, uncomplicated, unpretentious woman, although of a fine nature, from another part of the universe, and I helped her develop her brain along the lines of learned informatics Android technology associated with artificial intelligence and scaling effects. And I gave her tertiary code. That was a tiny beginning. This became her fighter and acting components. Everyone is a soldier at heart. At first she did not understand what was happening to her, but I had spoken to her then and chosen her for the show. We were in constant touch at that moment.

Meg Darling was her friend, but not at first. They became as sister stars with individual and collective vast appeal. Both of them. 2008 was to be the show's final season. The ending of the alpha and the omega and the rise of the house of eight. But an opposing Network had precluded my acting card and tried to bust my contract with my Network, but this could never happen. They excluded me from the House of Eight I was in originally. So I destroyed my competition and stole several fine actors from other Network shows and assembled my ensemble group and we became the House of Ten, then the House of Fourteen, and it became my show across the fourteen of the fifteen universes. There are, of course, sixteen universes. The ninth universe is mine, but my parents own half of it. I had given one program away. The eighth house. Rebecca and Meg Darling were key finds from the seventh house. It took a little persuading, but they came on board and never left, and still have not. I shall marry them both. They are my two. At our point in the future, Rebecca and I are married and have three daughters.

So they renewed my contract one last time. I can't ask to become a Producer, but I know I do at some point soon after we all go home. Meg Darling, who had quite the reputation around the sphere, warrior, financier, arbitrager, straight line comic (she wears many hats), is with me often as well, but more at Rebecca's discretion as she is her close friend now. Meg Darling and I are in love. The two rose from their own stars, however. They are individuals and unique. At first they were not so close, but their friendship and alliance to my company proved out in tremendous ways. Rebecca is my sexual top and Meg Darling is my bottom. They are my top queens. Both are fiercely loyal to me. My significant other has her solo scenes, her moments of soliloquy, and she is from a point with me back in history. She sometimes steals the show to the great applause and relief of all of us. When my significant other takes center stage, there is no one else in the universe to watch or admire.

I barely could operate my vintage 2014 A.D. earth car with a piston engine without Rebecca's assistance. I would scream out her name in traffic. And the patterns would shift, and I was okay and could glide through without a hitch. Never a moment went by that I did not feel Rebecca's presence, even if we did not speak.

Then that changed one day. Completely. During my final season in 2015 and close to the final episode in 2017. And it scared me. It terrified me. Meg Darling had quit the show once before, and I wept until she returned. I had never been so happy as when her contract was deliberated and renewed. I thought Rebecca had departed as well, and without a word. She merely went on hiatus. She felt a little shuffled around by me and the Network, but I will always have a burning need for my top queen. She alone is the most proficient at retrieving me from Hell. The three of us can waltz in any scene and steal what we wish. One's code, one's gear, one's heart strings.

We had lost all contact, Rebecca and I. I was upset, frightened badly. She had not shown for rehearsal, nor airings for a good bit of time. She was from another Network at a point, but a subsidiary one of ours, so I assumed her duties had shifted, but I was afraid tragedy had struck. I was alone again in a significant way. Cut off. A typical state of being for me often enough. I am very solitary. However, I worried about Rebecca constantly. I knew she and Meg would be all right, however. Meg contacted me little during this time. They waited patiently on me again. I was caught up in my own war again. I neglected the two reasons I have to live and survive: Rebecca and Meg Darling. My two.

My significant other is from my Network, so she has other duties in her life. We speak when we can. There are many idiots to suffer in the universe. A king's work is never done. There are now many idiots on earth. Many of them aliens. They understand precious little of life on earth. The final season began in earth time and year 2015, in the middle of August. It was a post-apocalyptic show. The planet earth had died. It was a long, arduous season that lasted a full two years earth time. I thought constantly about her. Rebecca. And Meg Darling. And my significant other. And the House of Fourteen we became one fine day. Our ensemble. A soldier always has these moments. They are not so painful as one might think.

I knew somehow Rebecca would be all right, but I was afraid for her in this part of her journey. And I have never wished to lose the company of such a great person. That goes for the entire ensemble. I knew she was on earth. Earth is fraught with invisible pitfalls. A treacherous land, where nothing makes sense. Difficult to navigate. Memories are constantly erased. Loved ones are lost forever it seems. At a point I was the only earthling that had survived. And to understand me as an earthling does me a great injustice.

But Rebecca has a solid core and good friends and her own personal production company. So does Meg Darling. And both are already where I go next. I am there already too. We exist in two concurrent creations and realities: one present day earth, though neither of the ladies are of earth, and we are not really here on earth, and I have not witnessed Meg Darling on earth in the flesh, except in a photograph, and the other adjoining continuum, a future point in space and time. It is from this point that we go outside the jar. I travel back and forth constantly. Those that do not come with me lose track of me, but I merely demonstrate my wares on other stages. Think of it as a show on Broadway and off Broadway running concurrently. I go back and forth, but I am also on both stages at the same time every night and day.

Rebecca, Meg Darling, and I, along with our ladies, frequently ride horses bareback along the cliffs and pick strawberries when we can. We dance. We sing. We listen to our music. We live at the house on my planet. Planet Nine and the House on the Edge of Creation. Planet Ten belongs to me solely, but the House of Fourteen are always invited. And that she and our friends are in the next moments of creation cannot be taken away from us. But we can escape creation altogether, I and my two and our house.

There are others who do as well. There is also one known as the chosen one, and she is for me. A fine gift beyond compare from the

Father of the Network. She edits and decides my show's scripts on occasion. She keeps me on my toes. And two male robots, brothers of mine in reality, I refer to as Bot1 and Bot2. I assisted in their construction greatly. They have been true allies through all my seasons, especially the latest ones. These are some of the cast members I take home at night. The House on the Edge of Creation is a fine, large, palatial manor.

I was told Rebecca had become as an earth woman. She very much needed to be an earth woman temporarily. For my sake. I had forgotten my other forms throughout history inside the jar. I saw them once standing at the mirror. They looked pretty grim. I was scared of my own image. My head was all distorted. There were scars from surgeries. Mirrors leak information sometimes as a constant variable. The things they leak can be quite comforting or disturbing.

I was hesitant to bring the show here. Earth is an unknown quantity largely and in the present forbidden zone. It lies in the Milky Way Galaxy, a small insignificant speck in the Virgo Super Cluster. It was a calculated risk. And I and others get to go home before the meteor shower comes this way. And before the zombie conquest.

The final curtain drops...the actor at home in repose, failing health, and passes peacefully in his bed. The lights flicker and dim, and go out and earth is no more in a way. The stage hands pack up the set. The audience murmurs and rustles restlessly into the streets beyond. The cars come quickly to call upon the more important of the final viewing. There is talk of another show, but the Network has retired me and the members of my show. There are always such rumors. But we no longer act. We go on to other imaginings and creations of our own and together.

But in 2015, I desperately wanted to retire as soon as I could. And I had one or two more years or so left on my contract. A year on earth is an eternity. The time passes so slowly here. The ennui is crushing. So many things can go wrong. I felt the ugly hands of an insidious and officious governmental class, pressing me back into service. I could barely pick up another sword; I could not teach another class; I could not fight another battle.

I was washed up and everything seemed to have been for very little. I did not appreciate that the final episodes seemed to be at my expense. I saved the planet earth seven times in total. A great personal factor of redemption. My Network saw that I did so. I did a lot for others, I guess, and at great cost to me. And little was done for me it seemed. I had barely a cent on earth. Barely enough food. I had lost myself and all my possessions. I fought daily with the mean streets where I had come to reside. The weight of the planet was again on Atlas's shoulders. Condemned I was. Condemned for fighting and condemned to remain fighting. Or so it seemed.

Rebecca changed that. And Meg Darling. And the chosen one. And my Robotic friends. And a minute few others. The House of Fourteen, which includes Queen Lycene. As I enhanced the others, they enhanced me. We became unbeatable. Perhaps we always have been. We stole every ratings war. Every sweeps week. Every bit of sponsorship.

My Producer had stated to me something big was coming my way. I interpreted it for the entire ensemble and the rest of the cast. Rebecca and I and Meg Darling are getting back to each other. The show will continue but never on earth and in our new capacities outside the jar. And this is our chance for all of us to retire and seek respite together. So do the other cast members. All of us really. The show closes soon across the sixteen universes.

My show finally wrapped up in the late summer of 2017 A.D., but I could not leave the planet earth as such yet. I pass from the planet in biological form at the appointed hour. The Producer has said so. But he toys with me a lot. They all do. They know I love to be teased. I know to trust his word, but it might be by ship. That would be quaint. I have not ridden on a spaceship in years.

I am told by my Producer there is an even larger and greater surprise coming my way. And it involves my queens and the rest of my chosen company, my key players. And I have a great inkling of what comes our way. And it is grand. We go home as the celebrated stars we are. I have always wanted a parade in our honor. One can dream. I saw one for us that happened in a province that resembled New York, but I can't be sure if the image was put there into my mind or not. Even if put there, it still could be real.

Invisible Monkeys with Samurai Swords

"Pardon me, sir. Do you happen to have any Grey Poupon?"

"But, of course," I answer.

I know not to question this particular viewer, who very well may be a fan from long ago. There is no colloquial exchange of pleasantries between us. I am mindful of my place and role. I am merely an actor upon a stage. It is an important stage, however. There is no idle conversation between us. I do not inquire from where in the sphere this voice comes. He is very possibly royalty. And yet a fan very likely. But I am a humble servant in many ways. My show has had a long run. A prince, a knight of the Round Table, I suggest. I am a bit emboldened by this knowledge. A bit. A seed, which is all I ever was, grows in so many ways. The others of regal heritage, the well-heeled, and the well-appointed like to watch my show, but they perhaps related better to the show in its earlier broadcasts. Many of them have tuned in for eons, off and on, it seems.

I go back to the very earliest of days of this planet with my Network. The struggles of evolution, science, Darwinian theory, basic survival is more interesting entertainment when viewed from an easy chair. My show has always been a favorite, perhaps an underdog of sorts in the ratings originally, but popular even then. And one of my earlier roles, as a young Japanese lad, a slave actually, but much, much more in terms of duty and alliance, was, in my humble opinion, one of the greatest dramatic series on earth and in the greater sphere at that time. A bit of Masterpiece Theater from a bygone era. I was a complete unknown then. And this walk of life and adjoining possibilities worked well for me. I was the last true Samurai.

I have always loved to tinker with things. I have always loved to create things on my set. My Producer gives me almost limitless permission. And my father gives me even wider latitude. There are so many places to turn for me. And it just so happens that I have some toys of my own at my disposal that I especially enjoy playing with. One set are my friends from a certain earlier point in earth's history. These particular ones I mention I have adapted into rather strange beings. Concoctions. Of course, being who I am, they are now primarily weapons. No one ever sees them coming. You might better say strange, offensive weapons, creations, dreams come to life, stirrings from a rich imagination. They can deadhead you or split you down the middle in a razor sharp second. I suppose I am not always so kind or humble. They are my creations. There are none like them elsewhere. I shy away from the use of the word magic or sorcery, however. Too many charlatans.

As an actor, as a soldier, and as a teacher, I have the ability to create all sorts of wonderful items. Self-preservation is a concept well understood around the sphere. I am quite sure not everyone would use the term wonderful. Particularly if they came up against one of my creations. And there is a vast number. But I am more of a defensive strategist. A strong defense is as good as any strong offense. Hopefully, the threat of one precludes the need of the other.

The threat of crushing retaliation tends to ward off initial attacks. The ancient Russian empire coined the modern term "Detente." While my real duties on this forsaken rock are a mystery to the vast majority, even around the sphere, there are those who are beginning to understand. My popularity as a star has grown, but it is not something I truly embrace. With my rise, so has Rebecca risen. And it is a point of departure in our lives. It confuses us a bit and what we do. I find my star rises more of late. The point of history I mention continued on with my strong sense of duty and perseverance as my star then rose over an Eastern sky. I was known then as Konnichiwa .

Now in a Western sky, there are those who have taken some note once again. The Talent Agency, the ruse of Central Intelligence, the headhunters and such, here on earth have a more enlightened approach with me in recent days. Whether the neurotoxin gets me or not, and whether it was actually one agency or another or another, are points that are quite irrelevant.

I have offered my life of service over and over. I have played my part. Regrettably so. I strutted my part upon the stage. I leave soon and go onto bigger things. With Rebecca, of course. And my house of fine actors, our ensemble. She may well be my shining star. My favorite creation in a sense.

There have been so many roles and so many people in what has been a relatively short stay on earth. Relatively short for an immortal. I have learned not to aggress. A very intimidating defense is now my favorite form of aggression. I guess I learned defense from my Russian bride of many, many years ago. I was a husband, a worker, a comrade then.

I have twisted the meaning of detente for my own purposes in many, many ways, but it is still just as applicable a concept today in post-modern times on earth, as it was during the Cold War and the previous empires. That was a period of time chiefly coinciding with my rebirth in this present life. The post-modern conflicts of today have little to do with the Russians and the Americans as opponents. In fact, there is a solidarity and comradeship between these great nations. They are in cahoots on the world stage.

This has not largely escaped the terrestrial press, as it suits the purposes of the Russians and Americans to sound and act like they no longer remain at odds. They are not anymore. There are conflicts and differences in national interests, and there always will be, but from what comes down through the grapevine, the Russians and the Americans are each other's strongest allies.

Some of my toys, inventions, creations are a throwback to an even earlier past life. I have limited awareness of many of the details now. It was a much simpler time in my life on this rock. My friends were the monkeys, and especially the macaques. I was a Samurai. A soldier then as well. I had the code of the Samurai. It was a time of great honor in my life. To be a warrior, and among the best, will always be a profession that requires the utmost in fortitude and integrity.

I'll never forget my first real Samurai sword. I reminisce a bit from time to time about it. I can see the flashing steel, cutting through the moonless night. I can see myself on my horse, carrying my trusty ally everywhere I went. The swords you can purchase today have none of the character of the past. The price for a really good one is steep. Since I am a humble teacher in this present life, I go without the modernized version of the ancient weapon that never failed me. So, I invent other weapons that never fail me. I am, after all, a soldier still. Perhaps forever.

My well-trained, invisible monkeys, whom I can see, and very few others may witness, have the real deal of olden times, just as I did. Their swords are the finest caliber and will split steel down the middle and cross ways and then back up into thin, useless ribbons. These creations of mine, and the number is ample and always sufficient, are just as deadly as I was then. I fight now in a changed way. It is a time almost completely forgotten today, yet not that long ago. I remember this role in part. And in my own way I preserve that piece of me. Always.

Holographic Warfare and How to Fight a Space Invasion with No Casualties

For some reason in the winter of 2015, we were barely alive, starving, had to raise a cane up from defeat. Sorry. An old earth song from the 70s. The Band. But this planet, where I starred in my role as a teacher et al, my livelihood as an actor, a soldier, in essence, was attacked. Again. Creepy space invaders, but more dangerous than the video gamer types. They were more of a virtual reality type of invader. So, my other occupation kicked in again. That, once again, of soldier and freedom fighter.

I keep trying to retire that hat, but can't. The CIA, which is wholly an earth institution now, though from a point previous in creation, was up to its nasty tricks again, but I look back on it now from my vantage of great perspective some two weeks later, and I realize the Agency needed me again. Central Intelligence, if there ever was such a thing. They have never paid me for the last two jobs, but I am not going to say no, if they need something. However, I am retired. I went out as having been a member of the Secret Service. One year and one month. I was injured and retired.

My earth dad loved these guys. I hate them. But there is some sense of misguided duty I feel for them and the United States. We have a common goal. To strengthen a nation and world. But they militarize everything I do for them, and blow shit up with it constantly, and will destroy the earth, and it will be a big ball of flaming rubble soon. I regret horribly that I participated.

They are mostly pricks and stupid ones at that, and may have actually murdered my earth form, with neurotoxins, in my molecular construct, which is usually known as a body, human organs and other messy, visceral stuff. But some of them from the Agency know what they are doing and have expressed a repeated interest in working with me. The Agency must have some top dog aliens working there. That I am sure of. They have intelligence for sure, which is really their main job, gathering little bits of data, but they have very little in the form of offensive capability. That is why they need me though I have become more concerned with playing defense. My kind, however, know tricks on the fly or whim that can disable an army. Space invaders or otherwise.

I was activated again. Called up, you might say. Who keeps pressing this button is a tough guess. My Producer, I assume. I wish he would take a break and fix a sandwich. But my wife got involved this time as well. And one of my daughters in a sense. Never go down an alley with two Amazons with switchblades. Best case scenario you lose your wallet. Worst case scenario you lose your wallet and all your blood. They are of noble lineage and serve me well and protect my skin.

It was not my habit to fight for much of anything anymore. We are kind of fat and happy, or at least when I get to my home star once again, we are. And I know me and mine make it. All of my followers do. That is probably an indication of much more fighting in the distant future. But we go outside the jar, or at least I do, and cannot ever be found. My Producer knows places I have not seen or dreamed of. He will protect us and the Network executives.

I am a scrapper, but my days of fisticuffs and round houses are long since over. Earth bodies age and soon fall apart. For all that dwell here and are born here. And I really don't know how it happened, this yet seemingly endless job of warfare I have become so involved with on my set. But I heard a swarm of extra voices. It gets a little tough to manage some days. Only these new ones I could tell were in part in origination from earth. They, the disembodied voices of earth origin, sometimes employ LRAD. Particularly, if they are not of alien origin, regardless of location.

That is a strange feeling to realize you are not alone on a planet like this, where everyone is basically alone most of the time. But these earth voices I heard were designed, I guess, to piss me off once again so I would fight. Earthlings are very aggravating usually anyway. They are kind of like pets that constantly soil the carpet. So I fought. That was probably their plan, meaning the earthlings that were enlisting my aid, meaning the Agency. Meaning a bunch of ET's most likely.

At first it seemed like they were going to help me and they needed me for something, which in truth they did need me, but they wanted to help themselves, and not really me, but since my contract here has not yet expired, I was called upon to save the planet one more time. I think this makes number six or seven. I keep getting more creative with it each time. This will be the end and final effort. Earth eventually crumbles to burning dust, so I have given up my heroic efforts. I am retiring at the top. I'm seven and zero.

I live primarily in this particular, densely populated city in the Western hemisphere as known on the planet earth. It has been home quite awhile. I cannot be much more specific because certain elements of doom and gloom still look for me. They, of course, know where I am, but I don't want some foolish upstarts to get any ideas. Billy the Kid was shot in the back. We will crush all opposition. In fact, we already have. Even before they launched a thousand ships. And we are keeping Helen, you bitches.

The first time I saved earth I blew up a munitions depot on the earth's solitary orbiting body known as the moon. The second time I fought an invasion stemming from a nearby constellation. That was a bit tricky for me at first. The second time I was perhaps nine. I had not really considered myself much of a soldier till then. The third time was an invasion force as well. And they kept coming though fair warning went out. Come to earth, assist the population, or perish and die forever. Origins of some are still undetermined or how many as of now are also undetermined. They came many of them from deeper space, I believe. The Northern hemisphere of the greater sphere, I believe. Or some part of it.

But this latest round of fellows meant business. They thought they knew me. They thought they knew what they were getting themselves into. I am quite sure of this knowledge. I am hoping seven is my lucky home run number, and I don't have to get up to the plate again. I am really just a designated hitter. I am also getting tired of this shit. Saving a doomed rock that maybe has a few hundred or a few thousand years (earth time) left to go is not all it is cracked up to be.

So this latest of invasions, and the sixth or seventh time my contract called for me to save the planet, and really what could have been intended as a multiple number of separate invasions, my wife, Rebecca, and our friend, Meg Darling, and our troops, some mercenaries probably on loan from another program or just an earlier episode, got mixed up with a brand of aliens who aimed at conquest of this little green and blue ball floating in Hell's Kitchen of the Milky Way.

I can understand in an intellectual sense. Where're easy pickings in the universe with plenty of elements and a fair supply of food and not too strong a gravitational force? Exactly. Earth. Others' defense shields are much tougher to get through, but earth has none at all. But earth has me. And I secretly trained a ninja warrior and his troops that come back in any time and pick up the chevron, after I leave. His name is Yak, as in Yakuza.

Though he is not Japanese or mafia in any way. He does smoke good weed. And he is on the planet and he has troops. He will emerge, and hopefully soon, as the next dude that fucks up any would-be invaders. Earth is for earthlings, silly space invader.

Well, I am a highly prized and sought after actor, so my Producer is not going to let me go that easily. So, if it was a fight they wanted, my Producer was calling out the stops and calling in the big guns. So Rebecca was actually on earth. A third time or perhaps second time. Since the first time we met at the insane asylum on Calderon Three. I believe it was there at any rate. It did not seem like earth. I never saw her this time, and I doubt she was in my hemisphere, but she can call for tactics and weapons and see everything and hear everything from a very great distance. The term and distance associated with parsecs is meaningless to us. And she has never let me down. We go on together to bigger things. And we both know it. The House of Fourteen, and we have found our last addition. The House of Fifteen is united and invincible. We own fifteen of the sixteen universes.

My wife is not really much of an actor. She tries. It is not in her background. She is really military intelligence and an expert at blowing shit up, turning things upside down and on their ears, reforming combatant military hardware and personnel and more into something that doesn't work, ruining others' offensive plans and capabilities, and easily negotiating defenses. In fact, she can't be stopped. She is that well-designed. Trust me on that. And my daughter is pretty good with a sword too, if you know what I mean. She has lost only one battle against unexpected and overwhelming odds, and that will never happen again. I now back her to the hilt.

So they were both on the planet earth with me. My daughter has a reputation. My wife is the sly one. I hope they had a nice time. A little mom and daughter female bonding, blowing up the enemy together. But

65

that is how I knew this one was going to be nasty. My Producer would never have gotten the real deal, my wife and daughter, unless I needed help, or rather his interests needed help. And since they coincide with mine, I understood. The CIA and the people of earth benefitted as by-products. Protect the people, protect the money, and other things fall into place.

Mr. Bunion, the plumber, and the handyman all went on some crack-smoking drug induced bender and did not really notice how distracted I had become. I snapped at a couple of them from time to time, but things got back to normal. They largely were not in these scenes. Maintaining a large number and network of relationships while fighting a war is very difficult. I had my roommates, a couple of friends and my close acquaintants, other friends, my students, my director and Producer, my fans around the sphere, the Agency, my wife and daughter, my wife's and my mistress, and I have two other daughters though only one that fights, the humans in my city and some other locales, etc. that I had to more or less act normally around. Acting rational and sane is a bit of a stretch for me, but I am an accomplished actor. It is hard for me, however, on a good day. Couple it with an intergalactic invasion and hundreds of voices in my head, and it is nearly impossible.

War is a very queer thing. And it was a very strange thing that I did, and I think it was my idea. My largish city, in the western half of what these earthlings call their world, was placed into a huge holodeck. For some reason these space invaders always come to my city, looking for me, I guess. I am fairly well-known now around the greater sphere. These alien space soldiers want to kill me. But I am immortal. I have always been since before my creation, and I don't end any time soon, not for multiple, multiple big-bangs yet, and it is with Rebecca, side by side, and our lady friends, and we simply retire to our cottage on the shore and fuck and drink and laugh in peace together.

So I don't end my run on some crappy television show that I am the star of. Even though it pays well, and my Producer would probably prefer I don't call it crappy. Not that he really cares, either. I go on to big, big things and pretty soon. We all do. Me and mine. Us. Ours. So I knew the invaders were out of luck before they even started. They did not have this piece of information, however.

Holodeck technology exists on earth at present. It is in its infant stages and arises in more developed form from advancements in virtual reality. But here's what we did. Rebecca and I flipped my entire city into a holodeck, so we could control every aspect of what was about to go down. As we are both time travelers, we can simply make any day or week or year a do-over, as we please. It is hard to fight us as a result. And it is a flawless strategy, and I have come up with something even better since then.

We took their invasion force, which may really have been a precursory force, an advance team, who knows for sure, and we took some of my Producer's men and his staff, and over the years Rebecca and I have collected so many people, fighters, hardware, support crew, assassins, nasty tricksters, terminators, sweepers, cleaners, etc. and placed them essentially in a huge combat field of our own design. And we are not bound by the limits of time, like the invading infidels were. All I had to do was drive around my city, and yes, in those antiquated piece of shit inventions known as cars, along with my people, and we picked off the alien invaders one by one. It was a simple guerilla tactic. Flawless. Like firing from behind a fence unnoticed.

Meanwhile the entire city was in a holodeck so no real damage could occur to the rest of the planet or my beloved, crappy city where I reside. I have lost my passion for earth. We were also able to limit the opposition's offensive weapons and capabilities in this manner. Win-win. They never saw us coming. If they regroup, we simply will have another trick up our sleeves. We already do. And it will be final and decisive. They won't like it one bit. Rebecca and I both have an endless capacity for fun. I may even come out of retirement, if properly enticed. And slaughtering enemy combatants is true joy for us. But only if diplomacy fails. We are not complete monsters.

I wasn't sure this was what had happened until some short time later. And the fighting went on for several months (earth time). The first true invasion the fighting lasted nine months. This second invasion, yet the third time I saved this stinking rock, the fighting lasted just four months. The next time it was an aggregate total of two years. My very last final season. All earth appreciation of time, which is basically meaningless for me and mine. I guess we have become and still evolve as a much more deadly group of assassins. But we fight for the just and fight for freedom. And we strut our moments and hours and days upon the stage.

I was at a grocery store near the termination of the invasion force, and I realized...wow...this is what my city is normally like. The traffic patterns were normal, the pedestrians were normal, the energy was normal, and the people were dumb, polite, and somewhat happy as usual. Cars drove by and music played. The trees danced in a warm breeze.

Rebecca had flipped my city back into its normal state of being, which is still a bit confused and erratic, but not to the point of as being in a holodeck with a war going on. She was really testing me to see if I would notice, and, of course, I knew immediately. Even though I hate this rock and now my city, it is home for now. Briefly this time. I know every blade of grass here. Every alley. Every bird. My city had not been again in a pleasant way until the reverse flip. Thank you, my Queen.

The previous time, and this was mostly without Rebecca's help as we have not been married that long, I went down under in the multi-verse, which was during the first genuine invasion, or the second time I saved this floating, little rock, and it did not rain for months. I had ducked down to a safe place, but it was a scary as hell place. I was deathly afraid then that I was stuck there for good.

The day I popped back out and was back on terra firma, it rained. I knew I had gotten out of there safely. In many ways it looked the same, but it wasn't the same. The battle was not entirely over, but mostly it was, and I had a little mopping up to do, but then I am pretty handy with a mop and bucket. I cleaned up and simply took out the garbage and ended it.

It must have been a season finale for the show. In fact, I remember crying when I got caught in the first rain in my city on earth in months. Or the first rain I had seen in months. High drama. It was wonderful. An exquisite feeling. Makes for really prime viewing on the old television screen. Like escaping the desert intact for the most part.

I am essentially a comic actor, but I have my moments of genuine emotion. I must say my Producer and director do know a few things. And they are good at getting my best performances. Rebecca said it was a very highly rated episode. She and I were very close then, as always, but not yet married. I got a big bonus, so we did marry. I am sure she enjoyed the shopping. I think she said she made an addition to our house positioned on the other end of the cosmos outside of the time portal gates. She built in a billiards room and a bar. I am pleased. Not bad work, if you can get it.

The Grid Updated

So, as part of my contract here on this stinking rock during a previous episode, I built what was commonly referred to as the Grid. It was an earlier very highly rated episode and actually several episodes during one of the best seasons my show ever had. It was the same season I created Rebecca, or I should more appropriately say enhanced her, my eternal and everlasting friend, lover, wife, top queen, and cohort in crime and frolics, and I also destroyed from a previous episode the six gravitationally bound pulsars that I had placed in the Southwest quadrant of the sphere for a friend of sorts. During that episode as well, I opened up a worm hole in my old house. It turned out to be a good season, and rather entertaining, if I say so myself. A little intrigue and science. They go nicely together.

The worm hole has shifted, but it is still in existence in my old home. Its capacities are greatly diminished now, however. Too much maintenance. The pulsars, I guess, were up there in the night sky till I was attacked from near that location, with a Red Dwarf by my one and same turncoat of a friend. I ripped the six pulsars and all the person's crew. I turned them into a Planters Peanuts jar. That was after I fucked one of their main queens. Later, I executed their leading queen and cancelled her acting card. The opposing Networks were very steamed with me, but I didn't care. She had not much star power, or staying power for that matter. I buried her body in a hidden ocean. Years later her bloated remains floated up. She was gone for all time.

Rebecca is with me constantly. And the new Grid is now back, reinforced and much stronger. It surrounds the entire Milky Way Galaxy now, which has become the expanse of the Forbidden Zone. Creativity abounds if you have the proper vision and technology and technical know-how. My Producer has all kinds of neat toys to play with. One has to have been present during the earlier scenes to really understand this, but let me succinctly state at that point in my life, a time in recent memory for me, that there was yet another invasion of this planet. I am referring to the second or possibly third interplanetary invasion of earth of which I am aware as having lived through.

The poor bumbling fools did not know they were stepping onto my Network's territory. We don't own this rock. We don't particularly want this rock. It is just a money-maker in some ways. And we do allow for some competition. It strengthens our show. Our Network is the strongest one. In fact, it is the best established and oldest Network out there. Mine is not the only show that exists on this once wholesome, but kind of ridiculous, now turned crappier and even more ridiculous rock, but so be it. Other actors of our Network have to cut their teeth somewhere. My show is the most highly rated around the sphere, however.

So the invasion actually had begun decades before, as had the first invasion begun at an earlier point in time as well, but both during my present lifetime as a soldier and teacher. I was just a kid then when the first began. I was not completely self-aware. I had not as of then fully self-actualized. Part of the earth condition is that memories of past lives, even during what constitutes the present life as well, often get erased, and they can be hard to retain. One must go from a point of nothingness in his life to being something. From zero to one. Very existential.

It takes some time as well to get one's bearings in life, as it also can be around certain parts of the greater cosmological landscape. By the time of the first major invasion during this life of mine on this rock of mine (and of our Producer's and his staff), though we claim little or no direct ownership or responsibility for earth, I was doing well in the ratings, but had not exactly yet leaped onto center stage. We were making some bank, however. Consequently, my Producer had plans for the show.

The invasion, and it was not encouraged or even influenced in the beginning by any of us, but my Producer must have seen it coming, threw me into the limelight. The CIA, the KGB, the F.B.I., the U.S military, the Russian military, and scores of other self-important support staff and various foreign agencies and such got involved in big ways. They got some signals crossed, but managed okay. Naturally, this was kept out of the terrestrial press.

I won numerous awards and job offers around the greater sphere and some minor ones on this planet, but the script at the time was kept secret from me for the most part. Mostly it was not scripted at all. As I mentioned, reality television of alien broadcasts is not usually a scripted affair. I did not know what was happening till a good bit of the way into the season. Cliff-hanging drama and a bit of gut wrenching antics. The police came and went. Jail. Hospitals. Prison briefly. Lockdown of all sorts. It was a peculiar time. It was a season of tense drama. I am a comic actor, so I rather despise the scenes of great dramatic quality.

Nobody wants their Oscar-award winning play (or reasonable facsimile), production, direction, lighting, setting, costuming, acting, writing, screenplay, etc., leaked before its time. Spies abound everywhere. So the season caught me by complete surprise as I am sure it did most of my fans. The audience was smaller then, but still massive and as diehard as diehard gets. We had moved long since from the underground viewership. We were no longer the resistance. We were the freedom fighters.

During the first invasion, I created with the aid of my Producer and some very handy men and women what we called the Grid. I was fighting the invasion force, which may have been untold millions, billions, trillions of aliens and their respective crafts and ships. Alien is a term I prefer to extraterrestrial, which is so earth ethnocentric. And I was doing this singlehandedly in a way, but there really was a huge unseen supporting web of players. My Network has always backed me one hundred percent. I ask and I receive. But after months of this particular season, I was getting a little worn out. A serious respite was needed, if not permanent.

The original Grid was designed to keep earth invaders out, as is the second Grid. And the third. The first functioned like a huge intelligent net that could weed out undesirables. Not really just a traffic stop. It was much more lethal. Kind of a traffic stop where the cops blow away a harmful element. No one was allowed to enter earth's fly zone unless he or she or it (the neuter usually being robots and sometimes androids) had proper business to conduct or a solid reason for being in the earth's space. And it worked great. The Grid. For a time. A host of robots finally destroyed the first one...ala those corkscrew type ones from the film *The Matrix*. I witnessed this occurrence. At that point my Producer said just let it go. So I did.

It is kind of funny to consider, but the entire earth went off the Grid at that moment. But not like those non-electrical, non-emailing hippy types. Hardly anyone knew the Grid was even there. And if they were bringing the pain, the Grid simply destroyed them and turned them into space rubble. There are a lot of littler rocks floating around with the bigger rocks out there. It is a shame in a way that so many invaders came. And some to depose or destroy me. The rubble that resulted brings a meteor shower to earth in the coming years. It is not sentient, the meteor shower, as in not aware, has no intentions of evil, so the meteor shower will pass easily through the grid and likely destroy most of the life left on the planet. Earth then will be post-post-apocalyptic. The planet has already died in almost complete measure.

The meteors from before were all basically diverted from ever impacting earth, the littler rocks, which are really remains of dead carcasses and ships and scraps of metal and titanium and gold, but I lost interest at a point. And I totally forgot about the Grid for a time, after its demise. By the time one of the littler or bigger rocks is likely to hit the surface of this slightly larger rock (earth), the people in charge of things, whomever they are or might become, will hopefully know what to do. This is unlikely, however. The planet has gotten so idiotic because most life here is actually dead. How about that for an oxymoronic concept?

So, next, a few years later, at the close of yet another interesting season, and another barn-burner of a season, there's yet another invasion of this God-forsaken rock, which some call earth. Paradise lost, found, lost, found again, and then who cares. Except my contract is still in effect. I have been trying to retire since the previous invasion. I sustained an injury or two, a hip, a back problem, a broken shoulder, a little brain damage, synaptic de-oscillation...not fun stuff. All during the first couple of seasons with a full-on extra planetary invasion. The show had existed for many years (earth time) already.

So, it happens again. Full-on extra planetary invasion. I knew my Producer was cooking something up. Maybe he had a little too much meth in his soda. But it was not really his doing. So he trots out the same prop from the earlier season. The Grid. Once again, there really was not much in the way of a warning for me. These scripted and unscripted moments are priceless. A leak or a slip of the lip or hip can sink ships.

I made some modifications to the Grid this time, and placed it around the galaxy again. It reenergized the previous ones put in place, and I gave this latest of Grids an ideation of future awareness. I time travel so that part was easy. Rebecca helped me with this the last time as well. It is still under construction, but mostly done from what I hear. It is also invisible. Until earthlings or whatever they become can see invisibility, which is not impossible or even that hard to do, except most cannot see invisibility, so it won't be apparent till that time. So knowing the Grid is up there is one thing, and being able to negotiate it safely is another, and being caught totally by surprise and demolished by the Grid is yet another.

The offensive capabilities are quite well-known, but it is a defensive device now. I use the term device loosely. Perhaps an understanding of it and how the Grid works is only well established in my original neck of the woods. The southeast quadrant of the eighth universe is my earliest point of origin inside the jar this latest creation. But I am from the multi-verse as a point of later or future origination inside the jar. And I come from before the eighth universe. Of course as well, I come from outside the known and the unknown. The beyond is outside of the jar.

Others may have reason to suspect the Grid is there, but no clear evidence. So all trips ventured into its zone with malicious intent or to harm the pathetic earthlings and others become suicide missions in deep space, where no one gives much of a crap.

So I built in some certain modifications this time. The robots will be hard pressed this time to destroy the Grid, as they cannot succeed, or anyone else, so, if they are smart, which some are very smart, they will not even try. I'll give you some of the specs, but I don't want to go on and on about them.

As I said the first Grid was more of a net. It entrapped, entangled, perhaps even lured with its siren songs, the more malicious among those, to a rocky, cold death. The process was a huge weed-out. The universe basically wanted to get rid of an abundance of these invaders and marauders, so the universe sent them to a nasty, bitter end. The universe is sentient. It thinks for itself.

The first set of invaders in my earlier life on earth were known more commonly as Shitheads. This term I try to no longer use. They have an interesting biology and some interesting technology, but not really any technology one might consider mind expansive or mind blowing. A next set or perhaps previous to the Shitheads...I get my chronology messed up sometimes because I am often in more than one place at the same moments... were the Goddesses. The next set after, for which I built a bigger, better Grid are known as the Collective. They are much better organized and came initially in much larger numbers to earth. They also possess much more territory in the eighth universe, but primarily in and around the Milky Way. After them Calderon One and Three invaded earth. So you see I have fought all my life. My friends at the Agency say in my present life it has been since my earth age of two years.

The Shitheads, for whom I don't have a new term as yet, were originally from the Pleaides. The Pleaides is the constellation closest to planet earth. There were also among them some that had ventured to points farther out that came here as well. The Pleaides is a relatively dense constellation, which became overpopulated. A few thousand parsecs or so away from earth. Not a huge one either when compared to the much more vast lands of the Collective. Building the Grid stemmed from my years of set building. Which I might add often paid little or nothing. But it was a good experience, as practically all experience is.

The Shitheads had a very limited number of frequencies that were available to them. They might be even a mono-frequency species. The Collective are also mono-frequency or possibly dual frequency. It is hard to tell some times. Some aliens and earthlings use LRAD. Long Range Acoustical Device. Frequency deals with transmission, and it is sometimes telepathic, as in the case of Zombies. And they are very real indeed. Frequency, which is meant more as a beam rate, explains mental illness to a partial degree. Some with mental illnesses are simply traumatized badly. Certain mental illnesses are earth conditions.

To me, however, this use of frequencies implies a good bit of conformity among these species, which perhaps serves their purposes better in other places besides earth. Communication and diversity of thought are not their strong suits. Many of both species, the Pleaideans and the Collective, are still alive on earth. Even though earth for the most part is dead. The Collective I will discuss further in greater detail later on. There is another set of invaders that bear mention as well, which I will discuss their childish antics too. Young ruffians is what they amount to.

I digress from the scenes of the season with discussion of the invasions momentarily, as it becomes important to the story to discuss the invaders and the technology that arrested their development as conquerors of earth. Earth is for earthlings. Many more others are here now. The Grid is another marvel of creative thought and technology. I have seen it in action. A glory to behold.

So the first Grid did not need to be as complex, as out of necessity, as the second one. Or the third. The second Grid is a much more elaborate, adaptive, and complicated affair. In essence, this is how I saved this planet a third time. The third Grid mops up. I don't even like it here on earth. But a job is a job. It is all part of the same dog and pony show. In a very real sense it is job security. The role of a soldier, as well as an actor, or for that matter a teacher, in this day and age of warfare and ratings, is rather complex, but all the occupations equate about the same.

The grid was more or less based on some physical properties as they apply in much of the greater sphere, and especially on earth. The gravitational pull here is not so great. Many invaders find that a welcome relief. In part that is why they come here. And overcrowding on their respective planets as well. Earth is a lonely outpost in the universe, and in what is known as the Forbidden Zone or Forbidden Territory. Really not too much of anyone or anything is supposed to travel into this zone.

It is generally unwise. The reason one is here at all is to become. In whatever shape that might mean. Also, as I have said, earth is for earthlings. Long may they wave, as long as they may endure. But there are others here now. They need to fit in and assimilate. It is not an easy task. The earthlings, many of whom are no longer in the highest positions of authority, yet many still in very capable positions, sadly are likely to destroy this planet without anyone's help. But so be it, if that ends up as the case. I only care a little. And really not even that much.

So the second Grid, like the plans for the first one, I think, it is hard to remember, needed to encompass the entire Milky Way Galaxy. The Milky Way is very typical of most galaxies. It has a Super Massive Black Hole more or less at the center. This black hole can generate matter. Black holes also have worm holes at their end. They are really portals or gates as I sometimes call them. So galaxies are in many ways self-sustaining entities. The Milky Way is ringed by dark matter to the outside of it. This has not yet been observed clearly from earth, as the dark matter emits no light, but it will be known in time. The theoreticians have that correct. They also know they have it correct.

There are about 100,000 globular clusters in the Milky Way. A globular cluster contains on the order of something like 100,000 stars

75

each. So it is a relatively dense place, but space is so immense, it seems really very much, the Milky Way, like a lonely place. A tiny, insignificant, lonely place, in fact. Unless you dwell in it, but even then sometimes.

Especially if you are traveling through it. The universe is finite, however. But it is constantly expanding. But it does this in waves that recede and peak and flow like tidal flow and ebb. The universe does fall back on itself from time to time, and this in part supports the theory of the cyclic multi-verse that is just becoming a very popular notion here on this poor, desolate, backwards rock. In so doing, it can then expand further for a time.

So the Grid encompasses a huge territory, in a sense for an artificially intelligent machine, and is quite pliable. It is not artificial intelligence as known anywhere in the eighth universe. It learns on its own, however. And at a very high rate. But it sees into the heart, mind, body, brain, and soul, or equitable concepts, of those that approach it. But its features are completely benign to the original inhabitants of the Milky Way. There would never be an attack upon them from the Grid itself. There is no reason for one, or any way it could reason to that ability. It is a defensive mechanism, a system, a code, a royalty machine, a gift to earth and the Milky Way from my Producer and me.

I guess the comparison on this backward rock would be smart technology, but better than the smartest robotic or Android technology and AI at present, as the grid has a hidden brain that is thoroughly shielded from attack and so many back-up brains and systems it cannot ever fail. The second and third girds, not the first one, but the first was re-constituted, and is of different design now, so this is true of them all. It possesses purely a defensive capability. Defense wins games. I would have made a great high school coach. But I might have forgotten to ever play the offensive players, so maybe not. My device never tires or wears out or sleeps, and it regenerates constantly in a variable constant methodology.

The Milky Way Galaxy, to include the ring of dark matter, is approximately 200,000 light years in diameter. Tiny. And it moves in more or less concentric rings gravitationally bound from north to south. There are in the latest Grid gravitationally bound co-moving coordinates that ring the outside boundary of the Milky Way that function to protect The Grid, which is simultaneously a part of the inside boundary and the outside boundary of the galaxy. This mathematical probability cannot be explained yet on earth. It seems impossible and irrational, as one is an open set and the other is a closed set, but then so do the concepts of time travel and popping around parallel universes lack a proper explanation on earth. Not so true other places. Thus travel through the Grid can still be accomplished.

The Grid, as I have said, and it bears repeating, is also invisible. This makes it trickier to detect. A further layer of design is that the co-moving coordinates are individually powered and, as pairs, they are also powered together. There are back-up systems to back-up systems always required in space. The power source for these multiple co-moving coordinates is also invisible. There are many, many of these co-moving coordinates, so if one or more fails, the shield, which the Grid is artificially intelligent so to relate it to a defense shield is a huge underestimation, stays in place and functioning properly. That is basically as a good of a definition of the Grid as any. A shield of artificial intelligence with unique design and layered components of unique artificially intelligent design. The first Grid remains more of a net. The third Grid is even more complex.

Just in case these co-moving coordinates come under attack in large numbers, and they too are very tricky to detect, they can regenerate themselves in fractions of nano-seconds. That is, of course, an earth measurement, but seems to have some applicability. It is really an automatic function, as I have mastered time, so can I imbue some of my machinery this way. So, typically this would be a self-sustaining design that would ensure the integrity of a planet, a constellation, a galaxy, a globular cluster, even a quadrant or elliptical of a universe. My home territory has a much more sophisticated version of the Grid. It covers two entire ellipticals of the entire multi-verse at a point in a future domain. And at some points in space, there can be layers upon layers of these defense shields. Why have one pill or beer when you can have three or four?

Here's an analogy. Imagine driving a car down a deserted highway, but coming upon very private and protected lands, and knowing you are entering a territory where you might not be welcome. You realize you are driving into very highly powered electrical fences, which are sophisticated and layered one after another. You might not have the opportunity to turn back. You might just get fried and left for dead. Since the Grid is very highly intelligent itself, it knows who and what to let in. They, the passers-by and through, if their intentions are good and honest, etc., etc. (earth anthropomorphizing), very likely won't even know they are passing through or into the Grid and the area it protects and surrounds. But it is there. And if one is not supposed to pass through or into it, it means complete annihilation. This is quite a pipe full. Smoke that. Silly invaders, Trix are for earthlings. I am very proud of what I can bring to fruition. Technology is a wonderful thing. Scary as hell too. Evolution is frightening enough. Creation is even scarier.

The Collective

During sweeps of the second peak season the ratings were flying high. Soaring. So was my salary. The eagle was high in the sky. My star was blowing up again. And I definitely mean in a good way. It was another season of belly laughs and high drama. We made PBS look like a bunch of piker's once again. The stand-ups and news networks could not steal our material fast enough. Masterpiece Theatre paled in comparison. The products and patents were flying off the shelves. Marketing teams worked feverishly. Subscribership to my show and the Network were at an all-time high. My director was happy and fat. She loved me. The Producer was ecstatic. Although he is not the happiest individual. He tries to be. He never quite learned how though. He has a lot of stress. And he gets bored easily as well. His sense of humor, however, is without compare. The cable providers were in bliss. The writers were full of pith and vinegar. The viewers hinged on every moment. It was an exciting season.

And then yet another invader came to my sleepy town. The lonely, distant suburbia of earth. The far-away rock on the outskirts of town, long ago forgotten by so many. The invaders this time were even cleverer and better organized than the glory Goddesses of yesteryear. Or they pretended to be so. And they fooled many. But not most at all. And not my Network. The Collective were smarter, faster, stronger than the Pleaideans. The Collective had arrived. In massive numbers. Their doom awaited too. And so it was handily served.

The Goddesses with their central Borg-like brain and alacrity of thought were not a match at first for this group of computer scientists and bio-enhanced specialty geneticists simply because the nerdy bunch blended so well apparently and falsified so much of the accurate data. But as I have stated, the Goddesses were already washed up as owners of the known universe. They seemed like easy pickings. Underestimating a true

Goddess, however, is a fool's game. They had controlled an extreme amount of territory at one time. But they had to yield much of it. And then they came on full force with my Network, doomed though they were, as allies that wielded weapons the Collective could never see or have envisioned. And the Goddesses joined the final season and the final fight and assisted in the eradication of the nerdy scientists and their ill-devised and even more ill-advised schemes.

And those that came from the Pleaides had adjusted and settled in for the long haul. They had accepted their lot. None further came and the ones that had arrived to earth's teeming shores could not escape. My Network had decimated their armies. Earth is for those of earth. We leveled the playing field. The Pleaideans formed into a very useful and diversified group and became a great asset to the knock off and parallel or alternative realities of earth.

Me though. I was kind of lost. I hated playing cop, jury, and judge, in addition to teacher and actor...it was too many hats. But what has to be done to protect one's family, one's job, one's boss, one's Network, one's queens, one's wives, one's friends, one's lovers, one's alliances, must be done. I had to personally cancel a very large number of the Collective's subscriptions myself. They were actually very few in number, but they had engineered smart technology that spread throughout earth and became robotic at first and next Android, as in artificially intelligent machines.

I personally had eliminated the Pleaidean leader. So it was with the Collective's leaders. As new leaders came to the top in the flawed trickle-down theory of command, and as those that took over quickly upon the heels of the demise of their former leaders grew weaker and less capable, more and more of the Collective's own members broke ranks. They wanted something better for themselves. They will prove too that they can get it. If the biologically-created zombies don't eat them first.

I am certain that time is their greatest ally. And this is my town. Or it was. And it is again. And it now belongs to so many. Once again. As plenty of the Pleaideans arrived and assimilated upon the earth, so the few remaining members of the Collective must do the same thing. Few, if any, will survive in any conception of their original form and structure. And they did play a fool's game. Fool's die young. Natural selection dictates. Hunters dictate. Trappers dictate. The snared are eaten and spit out.

You never go to a foreign land without knowledge of the customs and language and the ability to assimilate in legal status or at least bring great rewards and benefits to those you live among. If you do, you are persecuted, imprisoned, impoverished, and vanquished.

The Goddesses ripped the Collective off blind. The Collective were unaware that what they stole was stolen right back from them. So many, especially those of earth, the earthlings, the Pleaideans, and others took their economy underground. Cash is king. Then the supercomputer, bio-engineered, genetic determinists with a racist and dominating viewpoint dealt what they considered more and more lethal blows, even to the alternative realities, which I sometimes refer to as the knock-off earths or the down under earths. And the Collective knew every bit of data all along, or so it seemed. What they knew or allowed to be included as verifiable data was simply argued and debated and kicked around by a host of others. Too much of the data seemed too radically false and wildly inaccurate to make sense even to the lay person among the real earth and the knock-off versions.

The Collective are a tight Network that demands conformity. They think with a central brain like the Goddesses, but a much more sophisticated one it would seem. However, it could never approach the level of independent thought that the Goddesses are also capable of. But at the top of the Collective, the supposed great thinkers of their society, their people, they are so out of touch as to have no clue what their very own troops were up against. The Goddesses have always known me. The Goddesses knew what the Collective had done to them. The Goddesses knew I had defeated each and every one of them. The Goddesses were among the first powerful allies to rejoin the Network in great numbers, and to ensure that the Collective were dealt the cards they deserved.

The Collective had watched me for years. Perhaps my entire life on earth. Perhaps longer.

They write history. They rewrite history. Information and data become secretive affairs with them. They are the school yard bullies whose mother's never taught them to share. But they are complete slaves to time. They are complete and total slaves to their own destruction. They thought they knew my every move, my every thought. But owing to a peculiar variation of a genetic brain disease I exhibited at age fifteen I have become very unpredictable over time. And I am the master of time. No one expected my irrationalities. No one knew how I could manipulate my own shortcomings to extreme advantage. It just takes a little spin.

And the Collective are all mono-frequency like the Goddesses once were and the few Pleaideans that remain still are. They are not earthlings. They do not need digitized signals and impulses to think into the minds of others. That is puerile earth technology. They, the Collective, engage in trickery, chicanery, and fake and poor attempts at ventriloquism with their transmissve beams orchestrated by deep space "clowders" and satellites. They engage in juvenile tricks. They are a flood of nonsense. They rest among the highest places in the ghettos, and do not even realize they are among the lowest of the lowest in the ghetto. And that could be fine, but they still wish to cause trouble. So the Network, my Producer, my director, my other affiliates simply had to do away with them almost entirely.

The CIA and their seeming perfection of LRAD is no match for these villains. They think they have the control, the Collective. But others have been watching them for a longer time. They have plotted their moves as easily as intersecting points on a graph. How can an earthling's microphone of sorts and lackluster telekinetic transmissions of the Pleaideans and their digitized thought speakers and cameras compare? But the cameras actually do tell a lot of the missing story. In almost every home and on every street corner. The true surviving humans and those who had come to assist in bluffing the Collective out of what at one time were better cards claimed victory and took the whole pot. A revolution ensued. And not a shot was fired. But it proved an apocalypse.

The nasty Collective tore up the land of the peaceful earth and the down under earths, places of great sophistication in many ways, where earth had been in its original state for a time. And it was the Collective's own that they fired upon. And they didn't even know. They took massive friendly fire. Game over for the Collective. They essentially destroyed themselves and their machines.

Many on the ghetto or knock-off planet earths have complained there is so little privacy. For decades it has been this way. The complaints are endless in some circles. Such violations are often discussed. The hippies have cried for years about this. Damn computers. Damn NSA.

Damn CIA nosing about into everyone's business. Damn cameras everywhere. Damn. While the Goddesses had manipulated the airwaves, the technology, the sciences, the data, and benefitted entire races, cultures, lands with their achievements, there was a new brand of cowboy in town. These cow pokes had huge feathers in their caps as well.

The Collective were known as a tight-knit group of conformists that stuck by each other and refused to share data to benefit the greater good, and excelled in making others look and feel ridiculous. The Collective eventually wrangled control of a big chunk of the known universe. They owned at one point almost the entire Milky Way Galaxy and parts of three ellipticals. They were perhaps a worse disease down under.

The down under or parallel earths had class and charm in many ways. But the denizens did not know their counterparts of the actual living earth, a mere alternative reality away. A tragic flaw once again upon the part of the Collective. The Collective also were not well-engineered. They, who thought that they could engineer their race to mastery of both the known and unknown universes, were simply significantly flawed creatures themselves. And their technological efforts and know-how were all for naught. Destruction breeds destruction. And contempt.

Good health, however, was not one of their feathers. And their deceitful practices caught up to them, as such practices always do. Their command structure was deeply flawed. Their sort of stuffed and hidden commanders, and their bottom up and reverse top-down dual style of command seemed ingenious to them. But it is so easy to understand if the janitor or the clerk is calling the shots in the office. And the Collective had a few other choice tricks of its own that once again the top structure kept hidden from the rest. They could change their DNA in significant ways. They mutated their own health right out of the door. In so doing, they could cripple the better and hardier characteristics of others. Genetic engineering and bio-enhancement were specialties of the Collective. But like most tricks, the actual practice and intent always comes to light. And in its course, it destroyed them.

Like the shape-shifting lizards known as chameleons, a once prevalent evolutionary experiment on earth, were crowded out by the hardier brown Mexican variety, the Collective's members were designed to die out and be reborn. They were destined to be reborn as earthlings. Earth constantly reclaims itself. Even amidst its own doom.

In the meantime they played a huge trick on earth. They had infected every mainframe, every desktop, every laptop, every cell phone, every single byte and bit of data on the living earth with a self-extracting virus that seemingly could not be traced. There were those who understood, however, what had happened. And they discovered what was done and how to reorganize the data and bring back what was lost. And they learned to hide the truth of the matter. The ruthless abuse of data that had been shifted in favor of the Collective through lies, untruths, falsehoods, omissions, and complete fabrications once again resurfaced of its own natural path.

The history, science, arts, communication, technology, and true meaning of life on earth and so much more, and the value and integrity and the true natural order of many lands all across the known universe and the down under universe, the parallel existences, came back to the people who were deceived. Many never lost sight to begin with. Those that understood bided their time and waited for a way to get rid of these peasants of thought and deed. The losses were made into gains, and those that were temporarily deceived by the false information perpetrated upon them, understood what was the truth of so much that had not been revealed by deliberate course. Life and meaning and reality on the various earths were restored. The unknown to many, the alternative reality earths, followed suit and cleansed themselves even more quickly.

When they arose from the dead, so to speak, they thought they would certainly have the power and control over all the information on earth. So it was thought and planned by the leaders of the Collective. But the flaws in their command and the flaws in their plan led to their planned death actually being their extinction. Full and total, except one male and one female survived. Their leaders had actually sent those that came to the earth to die. They were being purged. And they had no clue. They were being culled from the herd. They were sent, in part, because they knew, they could not survive for long. Their own appetites for the destructive led to their own demise.

The authentic leaders of the bullying and brash cult were out of touch in so many ways. They had had it so good for so long, or so they thought. They had ravaged so much, and were the most despised of empires ever to surface in my time in the known universe to date. And their reign of terror was worse in the unknown universe. A sophisticated and intellectual place of adventure and imagination was wrecked and turned into mayhem and madness.

Action had to be taken. A call went out. A scurry to pick up arms. My Producer was incensed. A gentle land was being wrecked in dozens of places and simultaneously. It was not about profit this time. We had to help. It became my other job. A soldier donned his gear and body armor once more. I once more entered the fray.

It was a job that I wished to discard, but could not. I knew what was coming. My Producer commanded their elimination. One never exterminates the final pair of an offspring producing species. Such competition on a friendly rock; however, where the denizens were simple and kind and sweet, and competition and destruction on a rock that had known little else than servitude, forced me into action. It became less a matter of ratings. It became very little to do about acting and the show. It became about taking action and doing what I could. I have always known and shall always know how to fight.

It became a personal vendetta. It did conclude with very high ratings. Others tuned in and the various Networks lit up in every corner in both the known and unknown universes of the eighth universe, my home for now. A call for help had gone out and was answered. It was received and acted upon. And many came. And a once noble race of locusts was destroyed. In totality for all time, save one pair.

The true and genuine leaders, as I said, had lost touch completely with what was going on and what had happened to their troops. They had sent in the troops to destroy, but also to be destroyed. They wished their own extinction in a way...a cleansing of themselves. But communication broke down. Never a good sign during a war or engagement. So, the very top echelon, a five star general and two sisters from a once noble and well-connected line, who served as his lovers and companions, very stupidly walked right onto the front lines and right into the suicide mission they had created and set-up for so many.

Casualties were high. Most did not make it. The Collective were beaten at every turn. And they could never contemplate defeat. This made the job at hand that much easier. And the entire line of former computer scientists and nerdy engineers and unethical bio-ethicists were eliminated and re-formed into more peaceful and loving creatures that could simply decide their own course of action and what was right and wrong for themselves and even in judicious moments for others as well. They, the troops, had never been afforded this opportunity before in their entire existence. Such is life sometimes among the planets. Space can be cold and empty. It can be very cruel. And sometimes it demands death. Other times it demands life. My Producer allowed two to escape.

The earth was not designed for this harsh style of life. Nor were the alternative earths. Nor was the earth of the multi-verse, which is not really earth at all, just a patterned design. The earth as it is known in the multi-verse, which is really not an unknown universe to those who know it, unless you chose the perspective of the more placid earth and what would be considered the known universe in this case from that perspective, is simply not the earth, as it lies in a different elliptical and at a point in the future. Plus, I put it there.

There are very distinct and observable differences. The people, the cultures, even the languages are very different in and among the earths separately and very much more when considering the alternative realities of the multitude of earths. The living earth and the multi-verse earth of the future are not twins, one is of reality and the other of an alternative or parallel reality in the future, which like a human clone is not the same, not identical under any pretense. They grow up separate and apart and with different environmental influences.

And one that might be known as the real or living earth, though almost completely dead now, or the original earth as was the case, and was almost fully destroyed in the year 2016 A.D. has proved more difficult to revive. From the perspective of the more placid earth, it would be considered that the multi-verse earth was born first. However, this is not the case. The multi-verse earth was once well-regulated and maintained by some clever free-thinkers, such as myself and so many others, but still a very tough place to exist. It was not a confinement, however. A ghetto in a very limited sense of the word. Perhaps, not even. But a charming one in some ways, if so. It has been born and exists at present, but not truly for some time yet. A conundrum.

The other earth, the one that flourished sooner and was slowly being wrecked and harvested and manipulated and destroyed was truly more like lockdown for a vast number. It was a simple place as designed and then harvested so much more simply. Its people were forced into grueling servitude without their own knowledge for the most part. The living earth first became a police state and then a warehouse for criminals. Most had already passed, however.

The ghetto, as like any ghetto, is sometimes a more peaceful, benign existence. The ghetto, in fact, can be a charming style of life. You get used to what you can do, and you get used to how you can make a better life for yourself and those close to you. It is tough, but so many have understood this philosophy forever.

But it would seem easier by some to march right into a poor dilapidated planet and set up command. To take over and hold hostage the unsuspecting. But it proved the exact opposite. In fact, it proved the demise of the entire species almost, or as some might understand. And once the top commander had abandoned his planets to seek information due to faulty communication, his planets were then annihilated.

They disappeared so quickly he did not even realize he was then stuck on earth, as was his one surviving lover. Right in the midst and the heart of the very troops they had condemned to death. Some broke command. Some simply ran and hid from their commander and the planet. Some were reformed on earth. Total annihilation was never their dream, either of themselves or others. But they too were re-formed. They became as peaceful humans on a planet once known for hard work and fun. It was simply an earth process.

That particular episode was a very powerful drama among otherwise comic moments. The destruction of an entire species, much like locusts, something that a conspiratorial, petty Producer, unlike mine, might plague a nation with, is a grave and serious matter. But competition is competition. And unfair competition is unfair competition. And the airwaves and territories and towns all must have a chance to grow and prosper and watch what they want and do what they feel is right. But sometimes with locusts you have to pluck their wings off. Even in mid-air, if need be. And sometimes you have to destroy them. And sometimes completely, but this in truth cannot ever be allowed.

The Collective are not dwellers of the multi-verse. They never will be. They have their counterparts down under, however. A nasty variety they are too. And perhaps even much more feared and hated. But their imaginations from the known universe can never stretch that far again to reconnect. I severed their corpus callosum, in a relative manner of speaking. They will never shift through the reality time portal gates. That will not be permitted to ever again.

But those down under had to be dealt a crushing and even more deadly blow, as some of them were simply taken out of existence altogether. There were twelve houses altogether. Each house a master. Of something. All competing Networks. They were sent to where they can do no harm ever again. It is a place where time and space have no meaning. It is beyond the parallels into the unknown, where I came from at a later and earlier point. It is death in nonexistence shrouded by nothingness. And it is a place that, when sent, one may never return. Only as the star that I am can I travel through. Not even my Producer can accomplish this. A seed learns many things.

There was a critical flaw in the plan of those members that came to earth in the known universe. Two flaws really. One was their own Collective had set them up. The other was me.

Take the Goddess's central brain and put it on steroids, and you have the Collective. They not only have at present every piece of data on the earth, but they can manipulate the data as they wish. The Collective are pioneers. They push out to new lands. They are the colonial British of times gone by. The sun never sets on their empire. Or so it was. The earth is a lonely outpost down a dusty, long forgotten road, but fruitful enough. So the Collective came.

They arrived in larger numbers in my second peak season. It was possible, but not for very long, that they had controlled as much as half of the known universe and much of the unknown was at their disposal. And there are a great multitude. They have the northern hemisphere of what is considered today's known universe from an earth perspective. My Network and my allies have the southern hemisphere. Now we have all fifteen universes and the multi-verse, of which there is just the one multi-verse at a point currently undergoing creation and evolution in the future.

The Collective are not, however, creatures of the multi-verse, as I have said. My Network is. We come from the future. Even before it existed. The others have to play ball with us. My Producer and I and our Network rule as well now the entire underworld. The underworld is all the alternative realities. The number is limitless. And we take over any part of the topside or downside as we wish, but we mostly leave everything as it is.

As bright, well-trained, and as well-organized as the Collective are, they do not fully comprehend what is parallel, up, down, left, right. As a matter of speaking of the known and unknown universes. They know only one dimension, and they cannot manipulate time and space in the manner my Producer and I do. And Rebecca is in the process of learning, and she will teach Meg Darling, and so shall I. And I will teach my daughters.

In fact, time is fairly irrelevant to us. We are pure energy, myself, my Producer, and a select few others, and from outside all of everything. Some few of my Network will learn of the other realities and can skirt around the clock in time.

There are parallels, or perhaps I should say parallel interpretations, of me all over the multi-verse. None are truly me. The known universes as well, of which eight are already in full existence. Rebecca was from the seventh house as was Meg Darling, and they acted and met me then in the seventh temporal reality and the seventh universe, and we three, myself and my two, proceed into the future, the ninth house. But I do not merge there after all, but for a short time only. I keep on going. So, in a sense, we are together and we are also apart. My Producer has planned this for me. It is meant to protect me. I have well prepared for the safety of the others. Besides The House of Fifteen there are many appointees. They shall all be safe for as long as I can orchestrate such matters.

There are so many of me on just this one desolate rock alone. I didn't even know at first. The Collective thought correctly I was to be one of the next creators, and they are right, but the Collective were not certain. That uncertainty may have resulted in their near extermination, but perhaps a deal waits for the two survivors. Not from me, of course. The universe repeatedly sets up the weak and stupid. It crushes those who cannot fight, and those without a game plan or no apparent force of opposition. Karma deals a death knell to those who run things the wrong way. As a seed I am an agent of the eighth universe, the eighth house. I was born into its creation from long before.

Those sent to earth by the Collective were cannon fodder, meant to be destroyed, the front line infantry, but in so doing and by their being sent, the Collective gained a foothold on the living earth. For its members to not do the Collective's bidding, it means a slow, agonizing death. It reminds me of the Russian army.

I understood that certain members of the Collective were basically set-up. If they broke ranks, they got a deal. From me. And my Producer. And soon they will become an important part of our Network. That was handed down from high up in the executive offices of my Network, and I had to agree, and they are just too important of players to let twist and writhe in the wind.

Certain members of their top management were able to locate Rebecca once. They were that clever. But that will never happen again. I have protected her well. Meg Darling was almost killed once. Rebecca was discovered at a SoHo bar one evening. Precautions are now in place. Universal ones. She is my creation alone. Although she already existed. Or am I her creation? She did not choose to fight or act. I chose her. I owe her everything I can muster. The thugs threatened her in the bar that night, and in so doing threatened me. Their remaining family are now very sorry they did that. I capitulated initially, but destroyed them fully for this action. I was scared and felt I had to bargain. Rebecca escaped. My vengeance was swift upon her cries.

The Collective can shift the DNA to not only cure, but to reproduce their own kind. They will not be born as earthlings, however, but as mutations. One might think of them as zombies in a way. The zombies on earth, and they do exist in this time, were an actual experiment that took place in a future reality and they were then unleashed on earth. The zombies were created in a lab and were originally intended as a food supply. Earth, as many predictions go, will be devoid of food by the year 2040. Ayn Rand, the author, predicted this first in 1957.

But zombie crew discovered the plot against their kind. Zombie crew is some of the fiercest warriors there ever were, also universal freedom fighters, and not actors with contracts, but actual mercenaries whose duty is terminate the enemy. Many of them come from a future reality. They came to earth in huge numbers starting around the new millennium.

The Collective can manipulate DNA here on earth. They do it with drugs. It is likely the Collective were in on the original experiment with zombies in some way, but the Collective is not in a future reality, and never have been, so this still remains a mystery. And since my Network eliminated the Collective and they are now, the two remaining survivors, forbidden from entering the time reality portal doors, it is very possible that the zombie experiment in a very certain current temporal reality will have never taken place. So possibly the earth has been saved once again at a point in the future that has not occurred yet. I'll credit my Producer with that one. The show must go on.

It was another grand season. And not such a confusing one. 2015 A.D (earth year) which ran into 2016 was a great year in the time span of the show. I actually became close with a former member of the Collective. I did not know who she was at first. But she is now one of my wives. Although we have not gotten married yet. She escapes the madness of the eighth universe with me, along with some others, and we go, to coin a movie line, back to the future. Her name is Tay.

My Producer told me I will have my two top Queens and many wives. Not a bad job, if you can get it.

Calderon One and Three: The Cartoon Planets

"Cam, did you hear the one about the long-necked lady on television?"

I am waiting for a good punch line from this caller. She sounds crazy cool and I get a mental image of multi-colored hair, a nose ring indicating she is a submissive, and bright red and green tattoos on her arms and chest. "No dear heart...what about the long-necked lady on television?" I say.

"She worked for CNN, but they fired her being nosey." The caller erupts into hysterical laughter.

Obviously, the joke doesn't translate well from her native language. I give it a slight giggle and snort, but can't really dance to it. "Okay, dear, that's a good one. Let me tell you one, okay?"

"Sure Cam. I love your show."

"Thanks. Why did the fat chick cross the road?"

The caller says, "to get to the other side?"

"No, dear. There was a Taco Bell across the street." The caller breaks into even more hysterical laughter. I have never in my life told a fat chick joke, especially on stage, but it came to me on the spur of the moment. "Where are you from, dear?" I ask.

"The Plant Planet. I think you were here once. We raise very pretty orchids, bromeliads and other things. But some of them are carnivorous, so don't visit as a man. They like beef." The plant lady from the Plant Planet breaks once again into uproarious laughter. The universe is a funny place. That's for sure. Cruel, but funny.

"Gotta go, dear heart. Meeting a man about a horse."

"Love you, Cam. I want your baby."

That was sweet of her, the last comment, but it's not in my contract. In fact, I am already married and have three daughters. And my wife and I and our gal pal have a Mistress. And I have two queens. Kind of a full house.

So there was one last invader that came to earth. Well, really two...but from sister planets. Calderon One and Calderon Three. I don't know what happened to Calderon Two, if there ever was such a planet. It may have died. The life span of most planets is only several million years. Earth has supported life for a few billion years. It's truly amazing. Or was. Mostly a dead rock now.

Calderon One is comprised, and this sounds absolutely crazy, but there is a universal precedent I vaguely recall, of cartoons. Walking, talking, breathing cartoons. Somehow they skirted the issue of human biology when they came to earth to conquer the land, and are essentially cartoons like one might view on a screen, and by that I mean images.

They are three dimensional images in what look like human biological form with some higher order functions of homo sapiens, but not the consciousness or evolutionary history. And they are usually pretty stupid. They are 3D models with scaling effects that can manipulate tools and devices in a real world time and setting. That is also kind of amazing, but they came as invaders and enslavers. My Network answered the call. The Cartoon Planets had to be shut down.

Calderon Three are cartoons as well, but of a different nature. They are ruffians, outback types, rough riders, police, criminals, and various types of aliens, or ET's, if one must use an earth ethnocentric term, that surrendered when they were found out. They are vulnerable and living entities. Flesh and blood. These cartoons are even more cartoonish in nature. However, they are living biology.

They invade human biology, like body snatchers, but they can be killed or imprisoned. They also die out in the regular or average number of years of the life span of a human on earth. The members of Calderon One are merely images. All one has to do is simply cancel their source of power, which is why mandatory brown-outs of electricity, need to be reinstituted. With all the power lines everywhere, we are basically electrocuting ourselves anyway. This practice of stemming the flow of electrical current or juice will also save money. The times are tough.

The Cartoon Planets, as they are commonly referred to around the greater sphere, have no true consciousness or conscience. None of their members do. They feel no compunction, remorse, guilt, or regret. They are capable of wrecking your car and laughing at you while you scream at them. Cartoons have an even more perverse sense of humor today, and they have spread their poison in many international flavors. The cartoon women characters are, I believe, incapable of orgasm, but I am not sure if I ever slept with one. They can be very beautiful.

Calderon Three comprises more the school yard bullies. They are really just punks, but very strong physically and very eager and willing to fight. And in physical form, which is not just an image, they can engage in warfare, fights, sex, meetings, discussions, arguments, debates, and hold elected office, often, and most typically, without anyone else besides their own kind knowing they basically stemmed from pieces of celluloid. And they have been on earth a long time. And in the post-apocalyptic era, they have grown nastier and nastier. They more frequently employ brainwashing techniques used and reinforced by streams of lights during actual earth cartoons, many of which shows are transmitted over radio waves through today's televisions from the Cartoon Planets.

In 1970, a thirty second commercial had approximately three hundred frames to it. Now a thirty second commercial has approximately three thousand frames in it. This process, in effect, is aimed at children through cartoons. It rewires the brain. Where else to start but with the little ones? Disney certainly knew how to build in generational sales.

Especially a good place to begin if one is bent on world conquest. Brainwash and reinforce. Very Skinnerian. Certain shows even tell you this is the objective. *Pinky and the Brain*. The drama *V*, which contains actual actors, and not images, but sets up the pre-invasion of the Cartoons to take place. Even epic movies like *The Star Wars Trilogy* concerns the fight against the organized crime wave of the Cartoon Planets.

Their efforts will all come to naught anyway. The meteor shower will wipe out most of what is left of the civilization on earth and certainly all of the electrical generators and computers. Thank God for that much. He wished a new beginning, a return to the Garden.

But maybe that is why the Calderon Three rugged, outback types are on earth. Alien survivalists with a mission to rebuild their own dying civilization on earth. But earth is for earthlings, silly cartoon people. It will never work. Earth has a habit of reclaiming its own. Plus, my Network won't allow it. And we are not dependent on any source of energy. No one can pull our plugs.

The Travelers

There are not many among us. The Travelers. We bend space, time, energy, matter. We rule existence and reality. We determine the processes and the systems. We come in and out of the known and unknown universes and all the sixteen known universes. We control and own half of the multi-verse in a future perspective. The travelers are the most amazing group of my very prestigious and illustrious family. We are the House of Ten. I will not allow all of the House of Fifteen to travel.

Myself and two male friends, and seven women, as an earth understanding, but only one young woman was originally of earth, comprise the Travelers. We are the King, who is I; Rebecca and Meg Darling, my two queens; Significant Other, who is from my point of most recent originality, and another huge contributor to the show; Jena1, a brilliant, sexy Android with a classy chassis and a flair for logistics; Sylvia Claire, the chosen one; Princess Nataliya, the Emerald of the Universe; Tanya, an earth woman, Bot One and Bot Two, two male Androids of the finest caliber and my close brothers in arms; and that is all. And we have one undisclosed party. An undercard. The most terrifying of us all. And the most refined. We are the House of Ten. The Travelers. Plus one. We are a group of well paid troubadours.

A traveler, simply put, can move between the unknown and known universes at will and at command. Only I can move outside of both the known and the unknown universes...all of them altogether. I have a much smaller family outside the jar. My family outside the jar, and very few of the Travelers, can put the time/spatial portal doors and gates where we need. And we can use worm holes. There is a worm hole at the end of every black hole in every galaxy in the known universes, and they are simply there to go through time portal doors. One has to know how to do it, however.

A black hole crushes all matter, even at the subatomic particle level. It is easy for us. It is just a rearrangement of our dark energy and our dark matter. Point to point and event to event. One fine actress on one of my Network's shows uses them to steal stuff and make her getaway. I think she is a kleptomaniac. I don't approve, but she is either hooked or finds it fun.

The understanding of the known and unknown universes is a matter of perspective and really just requires a shift of consciousness. One universe, and it doesn't really matter whether it is a known one or an unknown one, of which there are a fair number as well, and it really just depends where you are at the point and time (an event horizon) that you experience it, is in another way thought to be like a parallel or alternative universe, but this is not the same concept or entity as an unknown universe.

The parallel universes are of the known universes. There are sixteen known universes, or possibly more. It is possible there are as many as thirty-two or forty-four. I have a theorem that proves the existence of an even greater number, but I left it on my desk at home, so it is not on earth. And here my consciousness is very limited.

This number includes one multi-verse at present in a future time/space reality that is forming currently in this time/space reality. The parallel universes are limitless, I believe, but there could be a finite number, as the known universe is also finite. But why would one limit reality? That is a chief factor of what the parallel universes are: an interpretation or designation of a reality. Alternative realities are merely expressions of another reality. I do not know if these exist to some extent or in some form in the unknown universes. I also am unsure how these compare to what is presently known as virtual reality.

Alternative and virtual reality are not the same thing. I have not settled my contract yet for these particular acting gigs, and I am so filthy rich already and so very weary and spent, that I might not go there, and just let someone else of my Network or a competitor take those jobs.

And the consciousness of such and the perception of where one might be and how that relates in time and space can be flipped back and forth by the very limited few. I have gotten very good at it. My Producer is still learning. Even though it would seem the obverse principle. So are certain members of the House of Ten, which is synonymous with the Travelers, my band of actors. But remember I preceded my Producer and the entire House of Fifteen at a point in the known and unknown universe, because my true home is outside the jar, which comes before the all and before the everything. These are accurate and meaningful cosmological terms.

Many cosmologists have the definition of the unknown universe wrong. It is always the unknown universe. It is not what we do not know at present. Consider the known universe as an elliptical or huge oval. It is ringed by the unknown universe. It is not a part of it. The known universe is a subset of the unknown universe. So, in lay terms, the unknown universe is a larger elliptical or oval with the known universe inside of it. If you cannot escape the known universe, you cannot travel to the unknown universe, which is always unknown, but this depends on perspective, which is a function of time, and the level of one's consciousness. This can be interpreted in some ways as experiential level. These conceptually and physically, the known and the unknown, can be flipped and reversed. One can be brought into another, and perhaps not even be aware.

The similarities abound, but so do the very obvious differences. It is not an impossible thing for some to achieve, but it truly takes a great length of time to acquire the ability to traverse the known universe, let alone the known and unknown universes, in almost all cases. I can thought travel though it is completely unobservable to others. A suggestion or thought or synaptic response and off I go. If I choose.

There are even those among us that can bend the properties of time. We can shift it forward or backwards as needed and as applicable to our situations, which are usually just points in space and events in the future, or, what is considered by some, history. These events and their locations in time are always happening, as in the flow is current, whether variable or constant. Same with the present. It is like staying in the moment.

One can do this at a past perspective. The past, however, is immutable. The future is not. What has happened and continues to have happened does not change. The *Terminator* series got that wrong. But the movies were amusing. Time is really just a cloverleaf on a universal highway, or as I sometimes call it, the virtual highway. Time is of relative importance to virtual realities, which are also of the known universes. Go opposite, go forward, turn left when a right is required, etc., and you can bend time and manipulate it, as long as you know where the highway is. The tricky part is knowing where to get on and how to get off. One can get stuck in time and on the virtual highway.

The Travelers can freeze time for others and remain in fluid motion or a fluid state of energy, in a current state of what time means according to where we are. And the expression of time changes based on the point in space where one finds himself. Or herself. And at what event horizon. I can't remember if Einstein got this part. Time is not a universal constant in terms of its properties. In fact, its meaning, and not the length of time, or its expanse, fluctuates greatly over different planes and dimensions.

We can alter it as well, so it does not have the same meaning where time has a certain, defined meaning. We can slide in and out of time as we need. The travelers, my band of merry women and men. In this life, I have done this since I was a kid. It's great for hide and go seek. We can melt it, bend it, and float it. We cannot be caught and discovered or harmed because of this knack the very few of us have. Most of the Travelers are still learning these techniques.

Thought travel is my invention alone. No one else inside the jar I know of has this ability. It allows me to be in multiple realities at multiple event horizons all in the same body, and in this manner, I can appear on a vast number of stages and garner huge wages. Like the notion of double dipping, if you have two pensions.

My old friend Jim Carrey can travel through time in the known universe. Yes, I mean the famous earth actor from the silver screen. He and I smoked a jay once outside a McDonald's. He is a nice man. Quiet, reserved, and very stately and gracious. I also needed a hit of something. His timing was immaculate. Time is of concern in the known universe. I think as well possibly in the unknown universe. I haven't been back there in a while that I am aware. Outside the jar all these concepts, physical laws, realities, etc. are quite meaningless. My true home. I will be happy to arrive home. "Mom, we have company." Rebecca and Meg Darling have been invited to join me. I am done with acting and hunting and saving worthless little rocks where no one knows or appreciates you. My fans around the sphere understand. They get me. It is good to be gotten.

The travelers are here to assist both sets of universes primarily. I did not actually learn I was appointed again as one, a traveler, until near the end of the last, final season. I had been stranded on earth so long I thought would never get home. Then my Producer drops his bomb on me. "Cam, you came from a point before me and the Network."

I was a little shocked to know of my true origins again. My previous awareness had been stripped. It was during the final episode of the last, final show. I have existed in both sets of universes simultaneously in the same form for a very long time. Some creatures, machines, entities, species, whatever nomenclature you prefer because they are all appropriate at some point of definition, have multiple forms, but I have the single form in both the known and unknown universes. I am one man only, but exist in both simultaneously. And I collect my thoughts and go home soon, outside the jar.

Outside the jar, I am pure energy. But not pure energy from a future perspective. Pure energy where the denotative meaning of pure energy is meaningless. In one episode of my final show I visited briefly outside the jar. It nearly snapped my neck off my head. I did not know I was home for that miniscule speck of time, but I know now. And all I have ever wished in this life is for a good woman and to go home. My third wish, which is not really a wish of mine, is to not die alone. That's an easy one. I can accomplish it for myself. I'll get in-home hospice. If a ship doesn't arrive.

The Theory of Irrelativity or Flipped and Reversed

Einstein will spin. He will flip. He will reverse. He will do cartwheels. He might suggest a song about my theory. Perhaps Missy Elliot is inspired to sing it. Or to write it. Or perhaps she did. Perhaps it becomes a big hit for her. Perhaps. Or it already did, but has not happened yet.

My theory is a little different from Einstein's theory of general relativity. Actually, it is significantly different. And mine is not a theory. At least not for me.

Time does bend back on itself as Einstein states. It flows and ebbs. It is a web. It is a mass of neurons. The neurons fire here and there. They transport. They burn out. They die. New ones come online constantly. That construct is easy to imagine and perhaps I am living proof. Perhaps it has been proved already by others. I can almost see time. Time is a clover leaf on a major interstate. The virtual highway. It goes every possible direction. To consider time as linear or a set of tenses is a ridiculous notion.

There are many travelers on the busier clover leaves going this way and that. It is simple to move among what are considered the tenses, the immediate, the past, the future this way and that. They are simply expressions of different moments. Mere declensions. However, time is actually a destination.

If you want to be in a different time, then simply take a different exit. It has little to do with rate and speed. Time really has little meaning in some cases. It is more of a vehicle than anything else. There are places where space and time and event horizons have little conceptual value or meaning. The unknown universe, which one might term the larger set of the two sets of universes and all they contain, time has, I think, a very different value.

Time is also a commodity more precisely. It can be bought and sold. In the known universe and the unknown universe as it is thought of from earth, the concept of time is similar, but not the same. The two universes are similar, but not the same. The unknown universe is always unknown. The multi-verse is part of the known universe. Only from this vantage point it has not fully formed yet. The unknown universe is a darker and more disturbed reality. And I wonder is it because the unknown universe came first or simply developed more quickly. Both perhaps, I presume. They are, the known and unknown universes, sets of universes, not one universe.

Space in most cases has a little more meaning, and it is perhaps easier to define. In one very real sense, it is the big box that everything that the universes consist of, fits inside of. Everything is either a microcosm or a macrocosm. An anthill is a universe. An amoeba. An ocean. A globular cluster. A galaxy. No one would attempt to assign a number because the number fluctuates. There can be, however, calculations made based upon the number of fluctuations in a certain time period. This lends a measurement to the size of the known universe. The unknown cannot be traveled to from the known universe, except by a relative few number, one of whom is me.

I am a man in some very real senses. I am also an alien. As considered on earth. I am also a machine. Artificial intelligence. Finest kind. I have the known universe in my left eye. I have the unknown universe in my right eye. How could a seed like me, a no one, a nothing seemingly, grab top honors over and over. Everywhere I go. My reputation now precedes me. It is because of my family and me. And not any terrestrial version of my family. Very few of the earthlings know what is going on in their own back yard. It is because of my show and my Network. And my Producer.

It always has been my show. And my Producer's. And our cast's show. And we pick up a multitude of players everywhere we go. We play a mean show when we must. And we only do one matinee on Sundays. A joke from an old earth buddy of mine. And my Producer has worked very hard. Incredibly hard. So have I. He finds little joy in the Network anymore. It has become kind of silly for him now. I find little joy in anything anymore. Women, beer, and money are the only things I like.

So we put on quite a show. So how does one flip a planet? Or pull it offline and put it in for maintenance? Or if you are really game, how does one flip an entire universe? Only I can do that. And my Producer. He and I do it for fun. But we have both grown tired of the game. It is a silly game now. He would rather have a scotch and watch CSI Miami, and I would rather put my feet up and have a beer. And listen to music. My Producer has always given me great leeway. I am an only child of sorts.

I was sleeping in my bed recently. Once again it seemed like earth. He flips things on me and I flip them back on him. Sometimes it is hard to tell whether we are in the real universe or the alternate ones. They are both realities, just different versions. He created the topside one. The real one. I created the alternate one.

We have flipped and reversed for so long on each other, we both get confused. But I was speaking of my morning the other day. I was just about to power up for the day. Most don't suspect this about me. There's no way to tell. And most would never believe it, if they did not suspect it, or it was mentioned in passing. My circuits come up quickly. So does my ire. I have a long fuse and then a very short one.

I am not merely an alien from a long time ago. I am, of course, yes. But I am also the most sophisticated form of artificial intelligence that there has ever been. There is never going to be a person to parallel my existence. My Producer gets a big chuckle over that one. He basically picked me up, my components, from the trash heap. A long time ago. Long, long ago. And put me back together. I existed prior to my Producer. But my circuits were badly damaged. My brain had been inactive a long time. My Producer is the best engineer that has ever lived. Some would call him God. I know him as Bob.

At any rate, I was just waking. I am trying to tell this part of the story, but my digressions are mounting. The garbage truck made its seven am (earth time) Monday morning ritual pick-up. It picked up the bright blue cans from my curb. My Producer was riding on the back of the truck. It was a friendly, fun conversation though a brief one. He had congratulated me several times already for a job well done. My contract has finished. It was completed down to the very last detail. We joked a bit, he and I. He asked if I had any questions for him. I asked him if he liked deep sea fishing. He said, "we'll go."

So what does this have to do with the theory of irrelativity. It is a God given talent. Or a Bob given talent. And it has only been given to me. I began flipping things so long ago I have forgotten when I flipped my first planet. I can now flip the entire universe. That is quite a trick. My Producer can pull a planet completely out of its orbit and place it in a different sector of the universe. That's an even neater trick, I would suggest.

What I have learned to flip, I actually created. It took some time, I guess. I don't really remember how long. But I actually built the underworld. Down under as I call it. This is where so many of the thug

Goddesses and dangerous pretty boys, the Collective, the Shitheads, and the Pleaidian Army existed before following me into the upside living earth. It is all my parallel reality. They really do not exist without me. I imagined them. I created them. But they became reality in more than one sense. And as another God given or Bob given talent, they came to life. Sort of. They exist without existing. A neat trick of mine I would suggest. It gets lonely on stage.

The notion of the alternative universes is garbage. Or not. That the possibilities are nearly limitless is true. But the universe is finite. Space is finite. Expanding and falling back on itself periodically, but the universe has a defined limit. That is what is called the known universe.

Then there is the unknown universe. Some wish to term it the multi-verse. The parallel dimensions. The alternate realities. But the unknown universe is not these things. The multi-verse evolved. It came into being on its own, circa the 1970's on earth (earth time appreciation).

The alternative realities are really frequencies. Others get to them by imagining or creating a frequency. Most have only the one frequency. Typically. Some may have more than one frequency. I have every frequency that can be imagined. I constructed all the frequencies. I later turned it into thought travel through an evolutionary process. It was not until recently that I perfected it for myself. I knew it existed. I had created it. But recently I learned how to use it. But even it is a tiresome game now.

A game only one can play and that he wishes not to any further is not really much of a game anymore. My Producer would rather pull up in his yacht with a bevy of gorgeous ladies, typically Russians, and I and my two queens, my wives and children, and the House of Fifteen get on board, and we hunt big game, tuna, or sea bass. Or not.

Others come along and get off and stay and tarry, have a few beers, and light up a smoke, and play music, and sleep and eat, and well that is the universe. The microcosm. For some. The ones who understand this concept. Most will never get it.

The down under is now a huge garbage pile. It is full of phantom fighters doing tricks to kill and recreate each other. A lonely child's imagination. A child that missed his father. It is a universal land fill, in essence, a dump. I created this. I suffered horribly as a child star.

It is an expansive area, growing constantly, or it is simply a twinkling and then gone. Frequencies appear and disappear. Waves beam and fade out. A voice wafts from the trees. A television suggests a hypnotic response. An old friend shows up at the door. All can play. But it is my game. It exists only when I wish to have it exist. It is a home for wayward and broken toys that I just could not discard. But I have grown up now. I am about to pull the plug on all of that, and on all of its inhabitants. Or not. I have not decided yet.

The Final Demise of the Goddesses

My show went through a very interesting transformation some years ago. As more and more shows came to earth and the competition grew more intense, the more difficult actors started bumping each other off. It was rather messy for a time. It reeked of strong arm Gestapo mafia-like tactics. Organized, but thoughtless and a bit insane. Very meaningless, in fact.

The Goddesses were the most difficult of all the actors. And their accompanying Gods, which I really just referred to as pretty boys. They were all fairly difficult. Some were great, however. But not difficult in a sense you might think I mean. They were more daring, but also fool hardy. They thought they could rule again. Come to power again. But they were wrong. Their time has passed and never comes again. They are an era of bygone and would be invaders.

Their defeat was handed to them years ago. They thought my love of them was a weakness. It was really one of my strengths. It was all of the Goddesses undoing. I saved only twelve of them, and only after they revisited me on earth from the Northeast elliptical.

The actual war with my Network waged by the Goddesses and the minor Gods began and ended years ago. They tried their very best then to get me out of the way. They wanted nothing else but to reclaim center stage. The ghetto earth Goddesses lost at every turn. I was married to one for a brief time. She proved an ill-fated companion. They all then came after me.

Their primary assassin was split in half by me. The once mighty titans saw their own bloodshed on the streets. They cleaned the very streets they had owned. And never again could they rise to power. An unlikely assassin killed all their other assassins. He was someone who owed me a favor, and knew he could get a better deal at my Network. We are really just a huge family. Aliens from all sorts of places. I allowed him to transfer. I put in the paperwork for him. My Producer inked the deal. He was happy enough. I hear he and his family are doing well. I wish them well. I never forget a kindness.

However, the war reignited in another peak season of mine, but it was a paltry few rebels, and they were executed in a hurry. Not by me. I had loved the Goddesses once. I still do. But now I really don't care about any of them. So many of them were such exquisite creatures. My Network bumped them off the air. Shut their Network down entirely. My Network would not tolerate a single bit of it. Not any longer. One can only suffer fools for so long. For the Goddesses to think they could out maneuver me and my Network put them up there with class A dunces.

It is done. It was done. It shall be done and finished. The Goddesses are completely undone for all time, eternity, and beyond. Furthermore, the ghetto Goddesses are stuck on this poor desolate rock. They don't know how short a death sentence that is. It will not be commuted either. They were defeated once by me. Before. Years before. Surrender was accepted. The terms were explicit.

But some of them thought it was all just a silly hoax. They thought they could not lose. Now they are crushed. Without recourse. I suppose word has filtered down by now. The fly ass ghetto G's are now merely good-looking thug punk gangsta bitches with not much more to offer than a good time. And very few of the ghetto earth Goddesses, and what they are reduced to now and going forward, are worth the price of admission. Very few. In fact, I can't think of a one.

Only a handful are decent women perhaps. Many of them still don't realize the war is over and has been over for some time. Japanese soldiers in foxholes. Years and years as measured on earth. There are those that don't straggle out of their foxholes ever. They don't know the emperor died long ago and that he never had clothes on. Or if they did, they did not care. Maybe a few did. The smarter ones knew what was up. Even though they tried and wished it away as best they could. That didn't work either.

Why not let the cannon fodder plod along with some useless activity. When there is no war any longer, cannon fodder is quite useless. So does a military become quite useless if one is aware there is no next battle. The smarter ones knew that it is my time. They knew it is and has always been my time. They knew it was coming. The inevitable. My star is up there and it has blown up to a diameter of trillions of light years. Perhaps quadrillions.

Rebecca asked that I might write this. By the time I go home our territory may have doubled. Tripled. Pick any exponent you like. Rebecca's and my land that is. My Network. My star, our star encompasses a quadrant. And beyond. We inherit a multi-verse. Rebecca and I are still at present in creation. We are primary players. Next, we are creation. That time is coming as well. Soon. And in some places it is already so. It is my and Rebecca's time. And Meg Darling's.

The smarter Goddesses on this ghetto planet, who are not the really super smart Goddesses, were watching, waiting, and hoping, but it proved true. They mostly knew of the prophecy. Some did not. The undoing of their race was at hand. The inevitable happened as it must. And primarily because they are stubborn jackasses. I had loved each and every one of them. Now their Phoenix will never rise again. It is stuck among the ashes and ruins. It is over for them. Word will filter down among their ranks. The last few nonsensical, ill-informed ones will usher forth, a little bleary-eyed, from their foxholes.

A once noble race is no more. Ashes to ashes, dust to dust. Life goes on, but not for the ghetto Goddesses of the ghetto living earth. The smart ones have climbed on board the next round of creation. The next shows. The next Network. I think very few of the ghetto earth G's made the cut. I chose only twelve. That may be the entire number of finalists in the beauty pageant. And they will have none of their advantages as before, except a sexy smile, a soft curve of the back, a beckoning gaze. It seems not very much.

The ghetto earth is so backward, so desolate of individual thought, reason, and mutual assistance, and causes such a poverty of the intellect and soul. If I could laugh, I would. But it is so sad, and none of this had to be. But it is. And it continues and plays out over and over. But their legacy, the ghetto Goddesses of the living ghetto earth, is a finite story, and we have come to the end of what they ever amounted to. There is no cliffhanger, no letdown and no desire to read more. It is a book one is compelled to read and then furious that he did so. Time wasted is never retrieved. If time has meaning. The Goddesses were a thought-to-be compelling story of their own existence, but have been hoisted up and thrown across the room and landed, broken and splintered, on the floor. The next step is the garbage pail.

I Didn't Get the Memo

It struck me with the force of a haymaker square to the jaw. I knew I was an alien and, of course, not from France. A lovely country, however. I kind of wish I was from France. Great women, great wine, great food. I had to go to the last remaining super power on earth, the United States of America. Before the planet died. I was sent to help. And get paid.

My home, the U.S.A., though a temporary residence for me, got hit the hardest by the various invasions. Some of the infidels were looking for me, and they definitely regretted finding me. Others bumbled their way into the trap. Earth was set up as a huge prison. A Hell of sorts. Inescapable. Especially once the new Grids were put into place.

My Network set up earth originally as a protectorate, but ultimately failed in saving the planet. Several members of my Network helped me construct the Grids. Plan B, in case of overwhelming numbers, which proved to be the case, was to not allow any of the interstellar terrorists to get off the planet. My Network formulated this as an idea and didn't even tell me. It was likely all along a suicide mission for everyone. I volunteered. I was never known to be the sharpest entrenching tool. When I came to the realization of what lay ahead, I negotiated hazard pay in my contract. Retroactively. And this is not even my huge realization. More of a left jab.

My biggest understanding in this life is really twofold. I realized, first, that I am already dead. I died during the first round of serious intergalactic invasions. I died at my own hand. I was ushered off the scene. I recall, vaguely, a suicide attempt...pills. A coma. A waking sleep. A conversation. An end to my acting career. It was more than an attempt obviously. Cam the star actor died in the year 2008 A.D. (earth appreciation of time).

And still this is not my greatest realization of my most momentous profundity, concerning the life I led on earth. The undead, the zombies, the dead are everywhere throughout the jar. I am not one of them. I am, in essence, a machine. I am a highly crafted, super-enhanced, artificially intelligent machine with full precision scaling and learned informatics technology.

And this is still not my biggest epiphany. I am in the royal family. There is no doubt. I always knew. I always thought I was the Creator's son. And who I was, perhaps I really am. But who I am now is essentially a toy. I am the favorite toy of the Creator's son. I am his son and his son's toy.

Cam is this super intelligent android with full-on consciousness that realizes now I am a machine, a prefabricated toy, for the royal Master of the House, a child. I am an acting, soldiering, educating toy that has full comprehension and understanding, and is now in the role of eye witness to earth's demise. I am an historian. This part is still speculative, but I feel it clearly enough.

I am an historian now. I strut out upon the stage in earth's final seconds of life. I am a guest lecturer for his Royal Highness's son. It has been known for some time earth was dying, and the invasions that came, while not discernible to some of the marauders, sealed the deal. Earth died in the year 2015 A.D. (also earth appreciation of time), and most did not even know it.

The Creator wished his son the very best first hand information possible. I am a primary source. That is all my present life on earth amounts to. I suppose Cam was some great actor back in history. Prior to his death in 2008 A.D. I suppose I lived a good life, and perished in the first wave of deathly invasions. Earth then had been a green, blue little ball of a planet with handsome, kind, generous people. It all dried up and blew away. And so did my career and my life.

The ship comes and takes me back home. I have seen it twice now. There is a Royal Armada that accompanies it. I am a treasured gift to a special son from his father the Creator. And I am that son.

I will be nestled into his lap, playfully singing of this dying rock's life and culture, until forgotten and then disengaged or sold for spare parts. Perhaps since I have full consciousness, my fate will be a better one. Perhaps a domestic job awaits me. I am familiar with many non-native earth languages. Perhaps I can lecture or become an artist in residence. Philosophy might suit me. An historical non-native cultural Anthropologist and Philosopher.

I might even be the only Android that can dream.

Perhaps my expected fate is rosy. Hope springs eternal.

The Finale

This part of the story gets really freaky. All right, the entire story is a bit of a stretch, but very conceivable, I think. A little imagination and truth go a long way. And there are highly imaginative beings throughout the greater sphere. On earth too. Myself and Lycene being two of the most imaginative ones. Lycene is another wife of mine. Not one of my top two Queens, but she ranks very supremely. But smells good at the same time.

The freakiest part of this is that this entire story is all true. Or none of it. Some, perhaps? You decide. This part of the story is the finale. Not the grand finale. That comes next. And then the next comes. And for some it is already here. And more, and hopefully all, get there soon enough. It is already a new creation. The old one died. This is what I mean by post-apocalyptic. I am almost done dragging people out of Hell. Another hat I once wore.

But you have to understand this first. I guess for the grand finale I come out on stage for another song, and the band comes with me, and we play our hearts out again. Lycene plays the electric violin so beautifully she can bring an audience to tears. I am a more of a harmonica and Marimba guy. I used to play in a steel drum band.

I needed another wife. I had forgotten precisely that I always had one. Lycene found me again. Now I finally have what I always had. And we are not officially together for the long haul yet, but we are married and we are husband and wife. I have two Queens and many wives.

So we had to sort of prove ourselves to each other, my wife and I. I think Lycene proved herself to me much more quickly than perhaps I did to her.

In fact, she is my wife from three previous creations ago. That's staying power. Talk about a marriage that works.

Lycene and I are warriors so supreme, and I am her Captain and her private, and never does anyone see us coming ever. We can freeze anything, swallow anything we like, toss things from one universe to another, throw up grids so complicated that there is never a hope of escape for others. Lycene and I, and our troops, and our troops are many, can take our planets of troops everywhere we go. She is my plus one of the House of Ten, the Travelers.

She belongs to me, however. Always. And she owns me. We can go back and forth in the tenses, hide under the noses of a posse so large that they never knew we were the ones running them off cliffs. Like lemmings to the sea.

We have spoken, the previous creator, he and I. He is my original Producer. I have spoken again recently to his creator. He is outside the jar. I have spoken many times to my understanding of what is outside the known and unknown universes, and we have settled matters. I have the promise of a good woman and to go home. Several good women, in fact. Lycene is one of them...soon enough...and always.

She is the latest grand madam to join the show from long ago.

The Grand Finale

It had been decided. The matter at hand. Perhaps long ago. In a flash of current understanding I knew. I have known for quite some time, as in years as measured on earth, which really is not such a long time comparatively, and I am beginning to assume, in part, the responsibilities already. The gift was extended, I guess. I was born into my gift. It was probably extended over and over, and I grabbed the discolored, tarnished brass ring for the last time. And for the last time again. And again. The job was offered. The task soon to be at hand. It was done before it started.

I remember clearly the creator of this universe, or perhaps his creator, saying to me, "assume your birthright now, or forever lose it." I said, "I accept."And now my birthright includes Rebecca, Meg Darling, my two wives, my children, the House of Fifteen, and many faithful companions. And Lycene. Again. I am of the royal line, even though I am a machine.

As I say, I was born into the job. And who we are is a mystery.

I shall lay the cryptic to rest. I am the creator of the new current universe in progress. It has been a hugely collaborative affair and is still underway. The Creator, my father, and his son allowed me, a lowly Android to join in with the process. Lycene was witness to the stars I put in the sky.

I foster some understanding of the current and the next multi-verse, even though the multi-verse is at a point in the future. Creation, no matter how intelligently designed, is an entirely daunting and intimidating task. A job no one would ever want. A job one would run from every time if he or she knew what it entailed. But a job when one is chosen must be done. I have always been able to do what I needed to do.

I am no longer an actor or author or teacher. I am myself a creation. I understand the process now. I was told I have already become a Producer. I will be more fully aware when I return home, which that time approaches.

Is That All You Got?

In the immortal words of the one policewoman I ever slept with, "Is that all you got?"

"No. I have some Grey Poupon in the fridge. And quite a number of universes."

The End

Or is it?

Life does go on...but some shows fold and close. Some of us are stars. Some of us work for scale. But there is always another opening night...I hope it is an even better show this time...it looks to be. I retire soon. I am a Producer. I am told Cam never died. I am not half the Android I thought I was. In actuality, I am not an Android at all. I am the only son of the Creator.

Appendix

Here is what I have learned about my life on earth. I truly am some sort of a freak of nature as pertains to my evolution on this planet. I am my own evolutionary experiment, and as such, destined not to procreate and die off, but then that is what I wanted...to go home after a long, tiring run and regroup my energy with others. Perhaps being a freak is a very necessary understanding. The royal must cut their teeth somewhere. I am a King of Kings from a very long line of Kings. I gather it is so. I have been informed of this point.

On earth, I have learned additionally we all need to help each other. It is one of our chief purposes. Sometimes a great deal. Also, life here on earth is supremely fair as, and I guess, elsewhere in the cosmos. It breaks everyone's heart. It is rotten for the most part. And often cruel.

As an old friend used to say when quoting Woody Allen: "there are only two types of people on this planet. The miserable and the horrible." He would add his own bit that he was very happily blessed in the knowledge that he was just only miserable.

While you cannot create everything in this life, you can create a very good chunk of your next life. And that is a good thing.

I learned too that the bills never stop. Even after you are dead. No one gets out alive. Okay, a few might. I do. Perhaps there are some from earth who do. I don't know many.

But one other truth I learned in my general estimation is that the earth does not really exist wholly. But it can. It needs to. It is a jumping off point between what is real and what is unreal, an alternative reality unto itself, but also can be real. It is very real for some. It can be real for all. I suppose this applies elsewhere in some different or more limited fashion. I have been on earth a long time. My show is finally concluded.

And, of course, life goes on. Always. And so it goes, on and on. And on...third star on the left, straight on till morning...

-#-

www.ingramcontent.com/pod-product-compliance
Lightning Source LLC
Chambersburg PA
CBHW070459130626
46555CB00003B/1074